NAVIGATING STORIES

Published in Canada by Engen Books, St. John's, NL.

ISBN-13: 978-1-77478-003-9

Distributed by:
Engen Books
www.engenbooks.com
submissions@engenbooks.com

First mass market paperback printing: January 2021

Cover Design: Ellen Curtis

Slipstreamers Committee:
Amanda Labonté
Ali House
AJ Ryan
Ellen Curtis
Erin Vance
Lauralana Dunne
Matthew LeDrew

NAVIGATING STORIES

LISA M DALY & JD RYOT

PROLOGUE

A story:

The door was first found by Lamore. She was foraging in the forest and found a strange plant. She had never seen such a thing. It was tall, with stiff hairs, and most were topped with a tightly curled leaf. On some, the leaves were just starting to uncurl, showing the first signs of a feathery plant. It was new, and she picked a couple, wondering if they were good to eat. She found a concentration of them, and as she walked toward them, the air suddenly changed. It was a little colder, and a little heavier. It caught in her lungs, and she choked in surprise. Looking around, she noticed many of the plants and trees were different; many looked to be starting their first growth after the cold season, even though it was the hottest time of the year. Looking at her feet, she saw not only the coiled plant, but other unfamiliar plants just starting to push through the litter of the forest floor. Turning back, she saw only this unfamiliar forest. Stepping back the way she came, Lamore felt the warmth of the sun on her skin, and breathed deeply of the light air she knew. Turning again, she found her way back to the strange land.

Collecting some of the strange plants, putting them in her basket, Lamore stopped when she heard a noise. Voices, but in a tongue she did not know. Lamore stood and turned toward the sound. Two women came into the small clearing and looked at her. The women were dressed in clothes different from her own. Warmer clothes, better suited to the early growth season. The three stared at each other. Lamore extended her hands, palms up in a gesture of greeting, customary to her people. The women watched, and repeated the gesture and turned their hands slightly, opening them a little more. Lamore took this to be a greeting and did the same. Then, one of the women approached, looked in Lamore's basket, and removed one of the plants. She dropped it to the forest floor and crushed it under her foot. Then she showed Lamore another plant, picked a leaf, and put it in her mouth, chewing. The woman plucked a few more leaves and put them in Lamore's basket. Lamore understood. The plant she had was bad, maybe poisonous, and the other plant was good to eat. Lamore fished in her own basket and removed a handful of sweet berries. She offered them to the women, taking one for herself to show them they were safe to eat. The women each tried a berry, then took another couple, enjoying the sweetness. One of the women reached into a pouch on her hip and took out a small clay pot. Reaching her fingers in, she removed a soft brown substance. The woman took the brown and stretched it until it snapped. She passed a piece to Lamore, broke another for the other woman, and put her own piece in her mouth. Lamore took it and placed it in her own mouth, enjoying the rich sweet flavour. The three women took some time to go through the woods, the two showing Lamore the various edible plants. When they came to a wide river, one of the women stopped and built a fire, boiling water, while the other showed Lamore how to pick the green, curled plants that grew along the bank. They boiled them and ate them together.

Lamore spent the day with the two women, learning about the abundance of the forest. They would try to speak to each other, but Lamore could not make the same sounds as them, nor could they match her words. They gestured and demonstrated, communicating through movement. When she returned to the door, she had a basket full of treasures to bring back. Lamore wished she could communicate with the women about the door, but they refused to go through. Lamore left but returned the next day with a basket full of berries, plants, vegetables and dried meats from her own land. When she could not find the women, she left the basket in the clearing.

A few days later, Lamore returned to the new world. She did not see the women again, but when she checked the basket, her gifts had been replaced with gifts from the strange world. Then the harvest started, and Lamore could not get to the door for many days. When she returned, she had an abundance of gifts. The air was hot and dry, different from the chill of the harvest season. This time, the women were there with gifts of their own. They exchanged food, cooking utensils, cloth, and jewellery. The women gave Lamore a bracelet made from a hollow sort of quill, and Lamore gave them each a pin for their hair. They parted as friends.

Lamore returned each season. Sometimes the women

were there, sometimes others greeted her instead. Always they traded, sometimes taking the time to show how to prepare different things. As time went on, Lamore grew older, and took her granddaughter through the door. Lamore taught her what she knew of the world, took her to the river, majestic in a different way from their own ocean. The granddaughter learned, and, over time, met people from the other world, and traded. The granddaughter took her own child to learn of the new world.

Generations passed and the worlds changed. Technology changes in this world and that. Our world discovered halfstone and theirs discovered a black belching energy. Our capital grows large, and in theirs, homes and buildings appear along the river. The people we trade with change, but stay the same. The language changes, but it remains impossible to speak. In their cold months, their people start to brave our world, looking for warmth and shelter. Their air becomes heavy and our visits become shorter. Finally, our people can no longer pass through the door, and those who come to us seem to have so little that we can no longer trade. But still, we give them shelter, and ask nothing in return.

CHAPTER ONE

Scritch, scritch, scritch, ting!

"Do I hear another artifact?" asked Jameson.

"Seems that way!" crowed Cassidy as she used a brush to delicately reveal the piece of porcelain.

"You always get the best units. How can I be only a meter away and not be finding anything?"

"I guess I am just lucky like that," she smiled as she picked up her clipboard and measuring tape. "It looks like another piece of that Delftware puzzle jug. I wonder if I've found enough to reassemble some of it." Cassidy started measuring the location of the artifact within her excavation unit.

"Oh, does this mean you'll actually be around for the lab work? You're not going to take off just in time for the 'boring' stuff, as you like to call it," Jameson teased. Unlike Cassidy, he enjoyed the laboratory analysis and the puzzle of the story told by the artifacts. Although cleaning the artifacts could get pretty tedious, he'd admit.

Cassidy wrote down her measurements and slumped slightly. She usually managed to find another project to avoid getting stuck in the lab and the library. Hours of cleaning artifacts, measuring and weighing them, and then typing them in the catalogues. Sure, reassembling the jug would be fun, like a 3D jigsaw puzzle with pieces missing, but there was so much to do before that. Picking up her camera and scale, she carefully took a picture of the fragment of porcelain, checked the image to make sure the blue transfer print was visible, and noted the photograph number. Why couldn't she just stick to the fun parts of being an archaeologist, like excavation and discovering sites? As long as her unit had artifacts, of course. A unit like Jameson's would be just as boring as the lab.

Dropping the artifact and label in a plastic bag, she sighed, "Yeah, it looks like I'll be stuck in the lab. You won't stick me with too much of the cataloguing, will you? Or the cleaning? Or the archival research?"

Jameson laughed, "What kind of an archaeologist are you? I know the lab isn't fun, but it can't just be finding things and that's it. We do have a duty to the job. Plus, this site is fascinating! I mean, at first glance, it looks like a major trade spot, especially with the variety of ceramics we've been finding."

"You mean I've been finding…"

Jameson ignored her and kept going, excited about analyzing the finds. "I think, if we work together and get the preliminary analysis done, which yes, does mean looking for obscure documents in the archives." He gave her a serious look, "You will help, right? I would like to get the first draft of an article out in time for the national conference. The whole team can get it out and hopefully help secure enough funding. This could be a multi-year project."

Cassidy rolled her eyes, "I'll do the work, Jameson. I know it's your project, but I'm just not as worried about the articles. And the students are much better at cleaning and labelling than I am."

"Well, you do tend to vanish, and never tell anyone about your projects. What is the point in archaeology if you're just going to hide all the information away? Don't you have a responsibility to the people you are researching? You won't even tell anyone what era or culture group you're working in."

"That's my secret. Like I said, I don't need the articles and the conferences–"

"Or the funding," he cut in.

"Or the funding. I just like the excitement of the finds. And if I don't need to clean and analyze," she paused as she uncovered part of the base of the puzzle jug, "why not just enjoy the finds?"

"You are living the dream, Cassidy. No worries about funding, and never having to present your work. I'm a little jealous."

"I know. It's pretty great," she said with a smile.

***

"Alright team, it's the second to last day of the season. That means we need to finish the excavations," Jameson looked pointedly at Cassidy, "so we can do all of the clean-up tomorrow. If your unit is finished, then help someone else. That might mean screening for others, or helping them with recording. The first two who finish their units need to help Cassidy with hers. That will mean measuring, recording, and using the fine screen for her dirt. She has a lot of artifacts, and some of them are pretty small, but we have been working all summer and I have confidence in your abilities. Okay team, let's finish the season!"

The team of archaeologists gave a small cheer, and dispersed to their units. Most were almost done and just had to finish their final few centimetres of sterile soil to make sure their unit contained no more artifacts. Cassidy would have to rush a little. The number of artifacts she found in her unit took time to record. By mid-afternoon, it seemed like she had ended up with four assistants, and together it looked like they would finish the unit before the end of the day. The rest of the crew had finished before lunch, and were doing the last of the recordings, taking soil samples, and drawing profile walls, plus photographing the site.

Tomorrow they would have to shovel all of the dirt back into the excavation units. They could all agree that tomorrow would be a tiring day, but Jameson had promised to buy a round of appetizers when they got back to the closest town. They had been living in tents for the past six weeks, three hours from civilization, so they were all looking forward to the pub. Some of them would probably have a few drinks, but it was a good crew, and they knew how to have fun without going to excess. There were a few non-drinkers, and they seemed to enjoy the social side of things (and the fried food). Jameson reflected that it had been a good summer, and a good field season.

Jameson was lost in thought while making field notes, when the satellite phone rang. Everyone on the site stopped and looked toward his field gear. He knew sat phones could take calls, but in all of his years in the field, he had never heard one ring.

"Hello?" he asked once he figured out how to answer the phone. The crew looked on, curious. "Um, yes, she is, just a moment please." He took the phone away from his mouth and carefully cupped a hand over the mouthpiece, "Ah, Cassidy, there's someone on the phone for you."

Cassidy dropped the last artifact from her unit in a bag and passed it to one of the students. "You folks can finish off this unit, right?" she asked. They nodded assent, still watching her and Jameson with the sat phone.

Cassidy almost skipped toward Jameson, her red hair bouncing and her grin spreading as she got closer. As she reached out her hand, he hesitated and said, "I guess this is your mysterious benefactor. And I guess this means you'll be leaving us with the lab work."

Cassidy smiled even more as she took the phone and said, "I can only hope," as she walked away to talk privately.

It was Dr. Herbert Gamgee, and indeed he did have a new task for her. Her heart soared as she knew there was no way she'd get stuck in the lab, or, heaven forbid, the archive.

A few minutes later, Cassidy returned to the site, smiling.

"So, I'm guessing from that grin you'll be leaving us?"

***

The next day started with the crew doing a few last minute sketches of unit profiles that had been missed the day before. Then it was all hands shovelling and moving dirt to refill every one of the excavation units they had worked so hard on. Jameson had Cassidy on backfill duty, while he inventoried all of the equipment and made notes about what was broken and needed repair, and what was completely beyond repair and would have to be replaced for the next season. He debated getting Cassidy to do this part, knowing how much she hated the paperwork side of things, but decided against it. Let her go off on her grand adventures; he wouldn't punish her for it. Seeing as he'd be using the equipment next year (as long as his funding came through) it was best for him to manage the inventory. Even if he *really* wanted to pawn it off on someone else.

Cassidy shovelled and dragged dirt across the excavation site. They had a wheelbarrow, but she let some of the crew use it while she piled dirt onto a tarp and pulled it across to the excavation units. There was always something sad, but still satisfying, to finish a field season. Shovelling back dirt was hard, but gave a wonderful finality to the summer. And it was that much better now that she knew she wouldn't end up having to clean the hundreds of artifacts they had recovered this season. She was thrilled to have been the one to find a few of those hundred: every fragment of ceramic, every pipe stem, every button was exciting. Besides her puzzle jug, she hadn't really found anything hugely interesting. One of the students had found a near perfect coin while Jameson had found a clay pipe bowl with an interesting stamp that would need further research to identify, which they were both sure would someday end up in a museum. Maybe there would be enough of her puzzle jug to also be on display, but she probably would hear about it after. Dr.

Gamgee was waiting.

They finished the site partway through the afternoon, and the team piled into the trucks and started back to the nearest town. It was a three-hour drive, and most of the crew napped on the way back, despite the eclectic tastes of music (Jameson favoured electronica, Cassidy epic classical, and another truck shook with heavy metal covers of pop songs). Spirits were high, and that evening a group of tired, dirty, but happy archaeologists piled into the pub. It had been a tough day, as last days of the season often are, and they knew the food would be hot and the drinks cold.

Jameson made sure everyone was seated before ordering one of every appetizer on the menu. After a month of canned food, oatmeal, and surplus military rations, hot, deep fried cheese and zucchini sounded like heaven. Everyone ordered drinks, and a surprising number of people ordered salads, craving fresh vegetables after weeks of wondering what exactly the "vegetable" was in the MRE vegetable pasta.

The drinks arrived, beer and sodas, and Jameson clinked his glass to get everyone's attention.

"First, I want to thank all of you for your hard work this summer. We pretty much kept to the schedule, and made some great finds. And backfill was done in record time," he paused as a server brought out the first of the food. "And I'm sure the prospect of greasy, unhealthy, deep fried food didn't encourage us to work any faster today," he chuckled.

The crew laughed, but didn't hesitate to dig into the finger foods. Jameson continued, "I do have some great news. Since we made it back to internet range, I learned that our funding has been extended. So anyone who wants two weeks of lab work, talk to me tonight or tomorrow. It will mostly be cleaning and cataloguing—"

"Which is the worst part of archaeology!"

"Please, no one listen to Dr. Cane."

Cassidy smiled as everyone laughed.

"But as I was saying, there is lab work available to those who want it. It's great experience, and those of you still in university, it will help you get work terms during the semester. Or help you kiss up to potential supervisors if you tell them you know how to clean, label, and catalogue."

"Wait now," Cassidy interrupted again. "I thought you were going to make me do this work. You never said anything about maybe more funding for the crew!"

"Doesn't really matter, now does it, what with you going away. Maybe, whenever you get back from whatever it is you do, we'll still have some cataloguing left for you," Jameson teased.

"Funny funny," she replied.

"Now, if that is all, Cassidy, I want everyone to raise their glass and toast a fantastic crew and a season well done. Cheers!"

"Cheers!" came the reply from the other archaeologists. Glasses clinked, and everyone drank to the summer.

Cassidy's phone chirped. She glanced at it, drank her cola, grabbed a fried mozzarella stick, stood up and said, "On that note, it's time for me to leave. Maybe see you next summer!"

"Only if you promise to clean some artifacts!" Jameson called after her. "Hey wait! You didn't pay for your drink!"

"Take it out of your new funding!" she called back.

Cassidy left the pub and got into an SUV idling outside the door. *It should be a jeep,* she thought, *like the archaeologists of the 60s, exploring the world looking for artifacts and hominid fossils in their jeep. But they never got to travel by portal.*

CHAPTER TWO

Cassidy loved campus. She hated studying, researching in the library, and long lectures, but she loved campus. Except for exam time, there was always such an element of excitement, especially near the start of the year. In the archaeology building, she wandered the corridors to her office.

Her office was small and cluttered. She had been at the university for a while now, and she could always see the layers of her time there. There were shelves covered in dusty folders of papers, maps spread across a table, books piled around the floor, and items Cassidy had previously collected. Those didn't look as forgotten as some of the piles of paper. For now at least.

Dr. Gamgee was seated in Cassidy's chair. When she opened the door, he stood and greeted her.

"Ah, Cassidy, it took you a while," Gamgee commented.

"Well, I was a day away from any town, so only a helicopter would have gotten me here sooner," she sniped back.

"Perhaps another time." He paused before continuing. "I need you to go to Fredericton, on the east coast of Canada. There's a portal where they used to have an airport," he handed her a sheet of paper, "here's a bit of background. I have you booked on a flight in a few hours. I hope you're okay with sleeping on the plane."

"After sharing a tent for a month, it will be okay." Cassidy glanced at the paper; it was a blog post about the airport, including the location.

"You'll be looking for a mineral. It has special magnetic properties and is important to my work. I need you to get a large sample of it," he indicated with his hands about the size of a carton of milk, "and when you get back, courier it to me, call it a scientific sample, or you might have trouble with airport security."

"Sounds good. Any idea where I'm going this time," she asked, not really wanting an answer. The surprise was part of the fun.

The physicist glared at her through his thick glasses, and turned to walk out of the office. She sat at her desk, looking at the printout about the airport.

***

The flight to Halifax was uneventful, but the one from Halifax to Fredericton was an experience. Cassidy did not know if she had ever been on a smaller commercial plane. Sure, she had been on short flights, just her and the pilot, but there was something strange about flying in the little Beechcraft. In private flights, she could talk to the pilot over the headset, and see what was happening. She had even been briefly offered the wheel before. This was different. Two rows of single seats, only seven seats deep, made up the cabin. There was no room to stow carry-on luggage, it had to be placed on a rack opposite the door. And there was no cabin crew. Before takeoff, the co-pilot came out and gave safety instructions, then went to the cockpit. The door to the cockpit was open and the passengers could watch the pilot and co-pilot work the instruments, but unless you got out of your seat and approached the two, they wouldn't know if you needed assistance. The engines were so loud that you would have to go to the cockpit because no one would be able to hear you.

Cassidy had watched one couple try to talk to each other across the aisle. It involved a lot of "what" and "I can't hear you". She put in her headphones, but could still hear the engines, and tried to get comfortable for the short flight. She watched the lights of Halifax disappear as they climbed through the clouds. With nothing to see, she closed her eyes and dozed.

She woke as the plane hit some turbulence. The blast of adrenaline as she was thrown around her seat made her fingertips tingle. Her phone fell from her lap and pulled free of the headphones as it slid under the seat before her. Cassidy clutched the armrests, her stomach lurching and her heart rate soaring as the plane dropped suddenly. There was no announcement from the cockpit, probably due to the older style of the aircraft. She realized just how comforting that a pilot's announcement could be during turbulence. She looked around the plane and saw the other passengers in varying states of panic. She looked outside. That was a little comforting, but she had to force herself to loosen her grip on the armrests and enjoy the ride. The plane levelled out, and the co-pilot turned around and gave the cabin a thumbs-up. Cassidy leaned forward and asked the passenger ahead of her for her phone, then went back to looking out the window, enjoying the feel of her pulse in her ears.

***

The Fredericton Airport was small. Small enough that they walked from the plane, across the tarmac, and into the airport. She carried her rucksack with her through the terminal. She looked for lunch, but the small kiosk in the airport was not appealing, so she found a cab instead.

"Welcome to Fredericton!" The taxi driver was rather friendly. "What brings you here?"

"Business, but first I'm looking for something to eat and I hope you can suggest somewhere," Cassidy smiled back.

CHAPTER THREE

The end of summer was still warm, but with a touch of the cool of autumn on the wind. Cassidy had a great meal of Caribbean food, surprised to find such a spot so far north. It reminded her of her last trip to Jamaica, and she enjoyed the lingering spices on her palate. She had stopped at a small convenience store and picked up some fruit and vegetables; something fresh to go with her dehydrated and MRE supplies. And chocolate. Always chocolate.

The taxi ride to the old airport was a little strange. The driver did not want to drop her off where there was nothing nearby, until Cassidy pointed out a house and said "That's the one! That's what my friend's house looks like."

The area was residential, not like the 1985 topographic map in the blog post. She was agog at how much the area had built up since the image. From the pictures, there had been a runway in this area, and a couple of outbuildings for the airplanes. The whole area around the airport had been farmland along the Saint John River. That was all gone and now it was a fairly dense residential neighbourhood; very different from the pictures from the 1940s and 1960s. Cassidy looked around, trying to see something that remained of the old airfield. She pulled out her phone and looked at a map of the area. In the middle of all of the backyards there was an area still full of trees. It seemed like an odd thing, this untouched grove, and figured it would be the best place to start.

She found a corner store set close to the grove, stopped in for more snacks, and walked to the back of the building, pushing through shrubs and trees. The undergrowth was thick, and there was a lot of litter and debris she had to climb through. The branches clawed at her back and pulled her red hair, but she forced her way through and the trees spaced out a little, making it much easier to move. Cassidy caught her breath, picked a broken twig out of her hair, tied it back up, and went further into the trees.

There was evidence of people having lived in the area; the remnants of a lean-to off to one side, a small fire pit and a broken frying pan. There was litter around the camp, and Cassidy walked in the other direction. It reasoned that the portal would be away from where people lived.

She walked slowly, between trees, trying to systematically pick through the area. It wouldn't be the first time she had walked past a portal. After about twenty minutes of searching, she felt the familiar disorienting sensation, and walked through to a new world, into a forest. Cassidy looked behind her, not sure if she had really found the portal, but she could no longer see the lean-to and litter, and the trees did look a little different. She stopped and listened, and could hear birdsong, not cars. Definitely a new world.

Cassidy pulled a compass out of the front of her bag. If this mineral had magnetic properties, perhaps the compass could help. The compass point wavered slightly, seemingly pulled in two directions. Unsure where to go, she pulled out a couple of pin flags, thanked Jameson for the donation from the field gear, and marked the portal. She turned back to the compass, and was distracted by a rumble and whoosh ahead and above her. Cassidy looked up and saw an airplane in line with one of the compass points. Decided, she started in that direction.

"Planes," she said to herself, "looking a heck of a lot like old planes from home."

Wandering through the trees, Cassidy noted that it was an older forest than the one she'd left. The trees were well-spaced and easy to navigate and she enjoyed the stroll. The weather was warm, but not hot, like spring. The air was clean, something she was used to from being in the field. After being at airports and then in a city, even as small as Fredericton, she took a few deep breaths to clean out her lungs. There was always something nice about fresh, clean air. Strange though, as she was obviously close to an airport, that she couldn't smell any sort of fuel on the air. Knowing full well she had a mission, she still took her time to relax and stretch her legs after her travel.

After about an hour of walking, Cassidy came out into a clearing, and before she could decide where to go next, a woman in long skirts and a light, flowing shirt, started to walk toward her with an exaggerated smile.

"Why hello," she said in a chipper voice, "it looks like

we have another one. My my, we didn't expect anyone for another two seasons, but here you are! I know you can't understand a word I say, but you're not a regular are you, so I'll keep talking and hopefully you'll know I'm friendly and won't run back into the forest. I'd hate for you to get lost." She chattered on, but in a happy, welcoming sort of tone.

"Um, I do understand," Cassidy interrupted.

The woman stopped short, her smile faltering for just a moment. "Oh, well. Wow. No one has ever understood us before. Well, isn't that just the insect's appendages. How?"

Cassidy smiled a warm smile, "It's complicated, but let's say a combination of magic and science."

"Magic? I don't understand that one. Science I do know! Well, this will be a slice of occasion bread. Come come, my name is Margaretta, and yours?"

"Cassidy. You don't seem surprised to see me walk out of the woods."

"Oh, tree flower, we get people who walk out of the woods pretty regularly. But you are a little early. The door people usually don't show up for another two seasons, which I believe is when your cold season starts. Then we'll have a group of visitors arrive for a while until it warms up again. We will often see the same faces over time, and sometimes they'll bring new people."

Cassidy was surprised. "You know about the portal? So much so that you expect people?"

"Oh, of course, of course. When the season comes, we go out to the door to greet them with food. They are always cold and hungry when they come through. But you don't seem either. It is very strange." Margaretta looked at her, questioning.

"It's a different season on the other side right now. It is still warm. Not as warm as here, but warm. And I planned to come through, so I brought food with me."

"You have food?! I would really like to try your food. Oh, I hope that's not too forward of me."

Cassidy laughed, "Of course not. I'd be happy to share my food. I think the people who usually come through are homeless, and must come through when it gets too cold to live outside. I noticed a lean-to when I came through the portal."

Margaretta looked confused. "What do you mean homeless? You mean without a home? Why would there be people without homes? Particularly with how hard it is to live on the other side of the door. We have people who live in shelters in the forests, but they can always come back to the town."

"There are long and complex reasons for why people have no homes in my world. Perhaps we can discuss it at another time? I wouldn't want your first conversation about the other side of the portal to be such a negative one," Cassidy said thoughtfully.

"Hmmm... yes, I suppose you are right. I have so many questions. And I must introduce you to the story-tellers. They will have so many questions, too. Perhaps not all at once, though. Would you like to eat first?"

Cassidy smiled. "Yes, that would be nice."

Margaretta laughed, "Then we will start with food, and maybe end as friends."

***

The meal was delicious. Cassidy couldn't recognize most of the fruit or vegetables, but instead of asking, she just enjoyed. It was one of the pleasures of her travel to experience food from everywhere. Usually it was a pleasure, at least.

Margaretta had led Cassidy to the town, which seemed to consist of family houses and a few larger buildings. Not surprising, being surrounded by trees, the buildings were mostly wooden, and a large body of water could be seen a little way past the buildings. A town on the seaside, Cassidy thought. As a contrast, every now and then an airplane would pass overhead. Surprisingly though, the planes were relatively quiet, especially compared to what she was used to.

"Oh, that's the base," Margaretta explained. "They set up last year. You see, the whole world is at war right now; not that you'd guess it from our quiet little town!"

Cassidy was intrigued. A base would probably have the magnetic mineral.

"I've seen the airplanes; we have something similar on my side of the portal, but ours are much louder. If a plane flew overhead where I'm from, it would be so loud that the walls would shake!" Cassidy explained.

"Yes," Margaretta continued, "we know about your, planes you said? I like that, shortening aeroplane to just plane! We got the idea from your side of the door. We always knew about the door, and now and then would visit."

"Have you been through?" asked Cassidy.

"Me, no. We have to be very careful going through.

Every few years someone will go through the door, but they can never stay long. Especially the past three or four generations. Your air is too heavy and too hard to breathe. It makes the lungs burn like a cookfire."

Cassidy contemplated this. The city of Fredericton had been around since the 1600s, but the railway probably didn't go through until the late 1800s or early 1900s, and the area itself wasn't really built up until more recently. In fact, according to the information Gamgee had given her, the area was pretty empty until the 1960s but now it was a residential area, and the whole area was much more polluted than when it was just farmland, or before that, when it was used by the Maliseet people indigenous to the area.

Margaretta interrupted Cassidy's train of thought. "We got the idea for the aeroplanes from your side of the door. My great-grandfather went through and saw the aeroplanes near the portal. He saw one take off and thought it was such a wonder. He went back a few times to talk to the people who flew them and to look at the machines. He figured out how to build them and took his aeroplanes to the capital where they began making them and making them better."

"But if they are based on our planes, how are they so quiet? Especially propeller planes. Those are incredibly noisy. I was just on one a few hours ago and my ears are still ringing!"

"There are other kinds of planes? Grandfather would be so interested!"

"I thought you said it was your great-grandfather?" asked Cassidy.

"Oh it was, but my grandfather helped when he was a young boy. He is proud of the aeroplanes, even if he is not happy with the base. On one side of the leaf, he blames the aeroplanes for the base being here, but on the other side of the leaf, he knows they are a huge accomplishment by his father."

Cassidy was getting a little lost. Margaretta had a lot of information to share, but she was having trouble keeping everything straight.

Margaretta must have noticed that Cassidy was a little overwhelmed.

"Let me get you set up in the visitor house. It's not really ready as you are so early, but you'll be snuggled like a crustacean. You can stay there until you are ready to go back through. Tomorrow, I can introduce you to the storytellers. Then we can tell you more. I know they'd love to meet you."

"That sounds lovely," replied Cassidy. She was going to have to take some time to regroup.

They left the eating area together and walked to a medium-sized house. The door was unlocked, and Margaretta led Cassidy inside.

"During the season, we can have as many as a dozen people here. We expanded the house a couple of times in the past few years, and might have to expand again soon. People are always welcome. We'll make space, but this year they'll be cozy, like seeds in a pod!" Margaretta smiled. "Pick any bed you'd like."

Cassidy walked to a bed near a window on the back wall and laid down her bag.

"Thank you, Margaretta. I didn't know what to expect,

but your hospitality is much more than I ever expected."

"It's what we do!" Margaretta beamed.

Cassidy smiled back, "I will take some time to think about things and make some notes."

"I will collect you in the morning for breakfast," Margaretta said as she closed the door to the house.

Cassidy sat on the bed and took out her notes. She had a notebook with the blog post print-out Gamgee had given her. Earlier, she had noted how what was once an airstrip was now a residential neighbourhood, and over the years, like so many Canadian cities, Fredericton had grown quite a bit. If the people here had been crossing over to Fredericton, she could see how they would have noticed a change in air quality. Hundreds of years ago, if it was just the Indigenous population, the air would have been clean, and still relatively clean with the first Europeans. As the city grew, there certainly would have been more pollution, from coal-burning steamships and trains to more people burning fires to heat the homes. Since the Second World War it would have been much worse. According to the information she had, the area of the portal was farmland, so probably not too polluted, but the railway also passed close by. The area she saw in Fredericton had a major road and a bypass road in the area, which would mean lots of cars, and lots of particles in the air. She thought the air was fairly clean, especially compared to big cities, but given the freshness to the air in this world, she could see how it would cause problems for anyone not used to it.

That brought her to the people coming through. Many portals had stories of people crossing through, but in this world, it was not only known but expected. In fact, they had used the portal to learn about new technologies. Cassidy wondered if they had been over to see the cars yet, and if they had started to learn about that, or if that hadn't been possible since the roads went through. They also expected people to come through. If they were waiting another couple of seasons, could that coincide with winter? When she was looking for the portal, she saw the lean-to of someone who was homeless. Perhaps some of the homeless population of Fredericton would pass through during the winter months. There were news stories every year from many cities about the problems of finding shelter for those without homes during the colder months, so could some know about the portal and use it instead of freezing to death? If the hospitality Cassidy experienced was any indicator, even being an unexpected guest, then it was surprising that they would only get a dozen or so people every winter. Perhaps it was a secret event within the homeless population so only some people would use the portal. And if they were homeless, why would they leave? Would they be encouraged to leave?

Cassidy was surprised at her own foolishness. Of course they would return through the portal; there would be the language barrier. Margaretta was so surprised that she spoke the same language, so whatever the language is, it must be absolutely insurmountable, even after generations of people passing through the area. The strange turns of phrase must be something that the translator had difficulty with; they sounded familiar, if not archaic, but strange at the same time. Perhaps it was taking the closest approximation and trying to turn it into something more recognizable.

That brought Cassidy to the mineral with magnetic properties that Dr. Gamgee wanted her to find. In the forest, the compass seemed to waver between two points. One point seemed to be toward the base, so it is possible that the mineral she was looking for was there. She would have to find out more about this war, and also see if she could visit the base and look for the mineral. She would also have to find out why Margaretta's grandfather was not happy with the base, and hopefully asking about it would not be a problem.

Now with a plan, Cassidy put away her notebook and laid back on the bed. It might be only mid-afternoon at home, but on this side of the portal it was dusk, and she had travelled quite a bit over the past few days. For once, it was a leisurely introduction to a new world, and she planned to take full advantage by getting a good sleep.

CHAPTER FOUR

Cassidy woke to the light coming in through the window above her bed. She felt refreshed after her travels of the previous day. She got up, rummaged through her bag for her toothbrush, and cleaned up at the tap and water basin next to the bed. Just as she was drying her face on a soft towel next to the basin, the door to the house creaked as it opened.

"Hello?" asked a timid voice. "Are you in here? Margaretta sent me. Daylight's up, so it's time to eat!" There was a little bit of excitement in that last statement.

"Yes, I'm here," replied Cassidy.

The door opened and a child, perhaps 8 or 9 by Cassidy's guess, was in the frame.

"Hello, I'm Cassidy," she said as she approached.

"Hiya! I'm Rim. Margaretta's meeting with the storytellers and telling them all about you. I've never talked to a forest person before. How come you can talk like us but none of the others ever can? I always have to act out stuff so they can understand."

"A while ago, I visited a place where they used science," Cassidy remembered Margaretta not quite understanding the idea of magic, but knowing science, "to make it so I could understand language no matter where I am. I have been many places, and no matter how people speak, I can speak with them."

"That's amazing! Can I get one of them so I can speak with the forest people?" Rim asked.

"No, I'm sorry, but I got it very far away and you would have to go back to where I live, and then somewhere else, to get it."

Rim considered this and replied, "No, that won't work, will it? Phia says it's hard to breathe through the door in the forest and that people can't stay there very long." Rim paused, then cheered up. "Did you know it was my great-great-grandfather who last spent lots of time on the other side of the door? He learned about aeroplanes. But now the aeroplanes are here and it makes my great-grandfather sad. He tried to go through the door, but said he could only stay a couple of minutes before he started coughing too much and his lungs hurt. He said the air is thick, like legume soup. Is the air thick?"

"Where I am from, it is not very thick, but it certainly isn't as clean and clear as what you have here. I have never breathed air this clean." She paused and asked, "You said your great-great-grandfather brought back the planes. Does that mean Margaretta is your mother?"

The child laughed. "No, silly. Jeanetta is my mom. Her and Margaretta are sisters."

"Oh, so she's your aunt?"

"What's an aunt?"

Cassidy stopped. They must not follow families in such a way, just looking at linear relations and not siblings. "Where I come from, an aunt is your mother or father's sister."

"Oh. No. She's just Margaretta," Rim said firmly. "Can we go eat now?"

Cassidy laughed, "Of course. I'm sorry I've been keeping you from your food."

Rim smiled and walked out of the house, expecting Cassidy to follow.

The meal was delightful. Once again, it was full of fruit and vegetables that Cassidy couldn't name, although Rim gave some names for the meals, and warned Cassidy away from some of the foods. Cassidy tried everything, and was delighted with the freshness. Anytime she had been in the archaeological field for any length of time, she craved fresh foods. That would often happen when most of what you ate came out of packages or needed to be rehydrated first. She couldn't think of a better feast than all of these fresh foods. She figured Rim was typical of most children she knew where they were still timid about new things, and had a laundry list of foods they did not like.

Rim also took the time, between bites, to introduce her to some of the others at the large breakfast table. While yesterday Cassidy and Margaretta had eaten alone, the community seemed to eat together. Cassidy had taken note of the long tables the day before, but Margaretta had been giving her so much information so quickly that she hadn't really thought about it. Now there were 30 or 40 people eating and talking. At the same time, while people ate together, they didn't seem to all start at once, as she noticed people coming and going. Even with the delay of having to collect Cassidy, she and Rim were not the last ones to arrive. Some people seemed to just sit and eat slowly, or even sit with a mug of hot drink; whatever Rim called it translated to cider, although that was not quite right. It was almost like a fruity coffee. Whatever it was, Cassidy was enjoying it, as were some of the others who just sat and talked over their cups. The whole experience was very welcoming and comfortable, not much different than her mornings out in the field where everyone ate together and discussed the plans for the day.

Once they were done, Rim showed Cassidy where the dishes went to be cleaned.

"In a few more seasons, I'm going to have to help with the dishes. I don't really want to, but we all have to when we get big enough," explained Rim. "But, it won't be many seasons after that until I can help with cooking. I've already done that a little bit during celebrations when they need extra help. I can help with cookies as long as I don't eat too many of them while helping."

Cassidy smiled. "So what do we do now?" she asked.

"Now," Rim stated proudly, "I get to take you to the storytellers."

***

Rim led Cassidy to an open building. It had walls, but large windows with wooden shutters that were all open to the bright day. There was a partial roof, but it was open in the centre, over a large fire pit. There were benches around the inner edge of the building, but still a lot of open space all around the fire pit. It looked perfect for community meetings or celebrations. Now, off to one side of the circular building, five individuals were congregated, some on benches and some on the hard-packed earth. Rim, having seen Cassidy safely to her destination, turned and ran away.

As Cassidy approached the group, she could overhear a little of their heated conversation. They may have been speaking in low tones, but the round room was obviously designed for noise to carry.

"What about this woman makes you want to share our secrets?" an elderly woman asked.

"It's the first visitor that we've seen that we could talk to, and she's very friendly," Margaretta replied.

"But we don't know anything about this woman," a young man said.

"So we talk to her," replied Margaretta.

"You're being too trusting, Margaretta," stated an older man. "I understand that it's exciting that you can talk and learn, believe me, I understand, but don't let a fascination with the other world cloud your judgment. She doesn't seem to be here for sanctuary. You said she's looking for something."

"So maybe we can help her," implored Margaretta.

"She's coming; maybe we should talk about this after we talk to her," said another man, just a few years older than Margaretta.

Cassidy approached the group.

"Um, hello. Are you ready for me?" she asked hesitantly. It was a little worrisome to know how they felt about her, but she was used to suspicion. It was rare for her to get to a new world and to be trusted so readily. Perhaps things weren't going to be as easy as she thought.

Margaretta approached.

"I hope you slept well," she said.

"Yes, thank you. The house is very comfortable," Cassidy replied.

"Good good. Let me introduce you to the storytellers. I already told you about my grandfather, Carlson," she gestured to a man with dark hair and features that were definitely similar to both Margaretta and Rim. Carlson nodded to Cassidy. He seemed like a serious man, with a sadness to his hunched shoulders. Margaretta indicated a white-haired woman to her left, "This is Gertrand. She is the oldest of the storytellers, with the longest memory."

Gertrand protested, "No, my darling flower blossom. You have shown many times that you now have the longest memory."

Margaretta blushed and mumbled a humble thank you before looking up at Cassidy. "Gertrand has taught me many stories, but I believe I have many more to learn." Gertrand smiled at Margaretta as she continued with the introductions. "Sasamuel has lived at the capital but moved here when he was Rim's age, and Olisker is the youngest member. He has shown to be a great storyteller, although he does have trouble keeping all of the ideas together."

Olisker looked down, a little ashamed, "Sometimes I mess up the stories and start telling one but finishing with another."

Sasamuel smiled at Olisker, "It just takes practice. Eventually you will be able to tell one story from start to finish."

Margaretta turned to Cassidy, "Together, we keep the stories of the island and share them with everyone so that we all know where we came from and who we are. We also find new stories that can be passed on. We write down the histories as well, but not everyone wants to read the books, so telling the stories helps everyone remember."

"I understand. We have many names for storytellers where I am from. Sometimes they are historians or folklorists, other times they are elders."

"Elders? Doesn't that mean old?" asked Gertrand, shock in her voice.

Cassidy smiled. The woman looked to be rather old herself. "It does mean old, but sometimes young people can have enough knowledge to be elders. Some societies respect the knowledge that only comes with age, while others respect a combination of age and knowledge that can be passed on."

Gertrand relaxed a little. "Good. I wouldn't want anyone calling me old."

Margaretta laughed, "Gertrand is only teasing. But we do not save knowledge just for the old. There are so many stories that much of a storyteller's younger days is learning them and practising telling them, and then in later years they tell the stories and teach them to the new storytellers."

Carlson had been examining Cassidy during the exchange, and spoke, "My granddaughter says you can speak to us because of a science experiment?"

"That is correct. I have travelled through many portals, or doors, in my world that have taken me many places. In one of those places, I was given a way to understand everyone else, and they to understand me."

"So we will be able to ask about your world? Will you be able to tell us more about the machines of your world?"

Carlson asked.

Cassidy remembered Margaretta telling her Carlson was proud of the planes.

"I can tell you whatever I can. I'm afraid I don't know much about how many of the machines work. I know some basics, but my work doesn't use a lot of machines, but more history. I look at things left behind by people in the past and try to learn about their lives," Cassidy explained.

Carlson's features lightened a little with just the hint of a smile. "So you are a storyteller," he stated.

Cassidy didn't think of herself that way. Between her work with Dr. Gamgee and the fact that she never quite stuck around any archaeological project to do any of the research and analysis, storyteller did not really seem to fit how she did things. But she was not going to argue, especially not if it endeared her to the group.

Sasamuel looked at Cassidy.

"What brings you here?" he asked.

Cassidy liked that he got to the point.

"I am looking for something. A very smart man, a man of science, but not a storyteller, sent me to find something in this world that can be of use to him. He has sent me to other worlds where I have located items that have then been used to heal the sick and to help people in my own world," Cassidy explained. "I don't always ask a lot of questions about why he wants an item," she confessed.

Olisker smiled, "So you like to be part of the stories! I do too. Sometimes I think they asked me to be a storyteller to keep me from exploring and adventuring."

Gertrand gave him a small cuff on the back of the head,

"Foolish boy. Storytellers need to understand stories, and all of your trouble," Olisker blushed a little, "means you know what it is to be part of a story and how to tell it. We know you told enough when trying to explain away your torn clothing."

"What is it you are looking for?" Sasamuel asked, bringing the conversation back around.

"I am looking for a mineral with strange magnetic properties. That was all I was told," Cassidy replied. "When I arrived, I used my compass," she took out the small device, "and on my world it is supposed to point to magnetic north, the top of the world, but here the needle wavers between two points." She reached out her hand, palm flat, to the centre of the group, giving them all a chance to look at the compass and see the needle moving back and forth. "The needle seems a little more focused that way," she pointed back toward the forest, "so I assume that is the equivalent to magnetic north. The needle also points to the base, so I think whatever it is I am looking for, I will find it there."

Carlson scowled at the compass. "Sometimes I wish my father had never told the capital about the aeroplanes. If he had never gone to the capital to try to make them, then they would never have known about the door, and we wouldn't have the base here now. All these people, destroying our quiet little community."

Gertrand gave Cassidy an apologetic smile. "I'm sure Margaretta explained about the base."

Margaretta looked down as Cassidy said, "No, not really."

"I'll explain," said Margaretta before Gertrand could

say anything further. "A dozen seasons ago, war broke out. We are just a small island, off the coast of a large country. There are four countries that control all of the land and all of the people. When two started a war, the other two countries were dragged in through treaties and the like. Now the entire world is at war. Our country was one of the first two. For a few seasons, it had no impact on us. We do not get many shipments from the capital, and we tend to rely on ourselves. There have been many times over the lifetimes where we have all but lost contact with the capital; usually when they are changing governments." Margaretta paused and looked at Gertrand, who motioned for her to continue. "Four seasons ago, military people came to our shores. They had great-grandfather's plans and were using them to make aeroplanes for war. The problem was, your 'planes' fly using a fuel that makes the air heavy, and great-grandfather, though he could figure out much, could not figure out a fuel source that would replace yours. He brought the plans to the capital, where they used halfstones as a fuel source. They also learned about the door. They have not figured out how to stay in your world, but they also want to make sure the other countries cannot go through either."

"That and apparently we are a 'strategic point of land' for the aeroplanes." Carlson's tone indicated he didn't believe that for a moment. "They're just using it as an excuse to keep an eye on us, and that damnable door."

"Carlson!" Gertrand reprimanded, "Do not talk like that. We help those who come through the door; it is a gift and has brought us many wonderful visitors. Sometimes, visitors have been a problem, but that door has been a joy to our people from the first stories."

"I know, I do. But that base has disrupted the hunting grounds, and they drained the wetland, which took away one of our most productive areas for collecting berries, and they even moved some of the graveyard! Imagine, digging up the dead just so you can build a runway," Carlson scoffed.

"It's better than them landing the planes on our dead, isn't it?" asked Sasamuel.

Carlson grunted in response, then went on. "And they've taken so many young people away from their usual work to work over there. Next thing they'll leave and forget the stories of where they are from."

"Hush now," Gertrand cut in, "you know full well our people have been leaving this island almost since we first came to it. And some leave and never return. They forget their stories and find new ones in their new life. But many others do come back, like your own father. The young ones at the base, many will leave, and some are even talking about going to war themselves, but many will also come back. It might be at the end of the war, it might be years later, but they will come back, and we will welcome them and share the stories they might have forgotten."

Gertrand had an authority to her. If Cassidy were to guess about how this community was run, she would guess that Gertrand was the one in charge, even if Carlson liked to think he had most of the authority.

"Cassidy," Gertrand addressed her, "you are welcome here. We do not know what it is you are searching for, but if it is to do good in your world, then we are happy to help you find it."

"Thank you," responded Cassidy. "Your support is appreciated."

Margaretta smiled at Cassidy and started to rock up on her toes, excitedly. Cassidy figured she must have passed whatever test there was in meeting the storytellers.

Margaretta continued excitedly. "I said before this is not when people usually come through the door. We usually don't have big events when we have visitors, mostly because we figure they wouldn't understand the stories, but we decided to invite you to a marriage this evening. Tomorrow we can worry about the base, but I hope you will join us." Margaretta was obviously very hopeful.

"Of course. I am honoured that you would have me," Cassidy replied. She was beginning to think that this trip might not be as much of an adventure as usual. She certainly wasn't used to having so much support, and, dare she say it, friendship, on her travels.

CHAPTER FIVE

The rest of the day was a bit of a whirlwind. This would be the first off-world wedding Cassidy had ever attended, and between Margaretta and Rim, she would be ready. Margaretta had brought Cassidy back to the visitor's house, and within minutes, Rim had arrived with a bunch of clothing. Margaretta had been confident that Cassidy would be invited to the evening's festivities, and had tasked Rim with asking the women of the village for clothing that Cassidy could wear. The women of the town seemed to favour long skirts, often of many colours in an almost patchwork style. These skirts on the other hand, were often a single colour, but had bright beading or dried flowers sewn in elaborate patterns. Cassidy tried on a few until she found a skirt that fit. All of the skirts flowed, and Cassidy could not help but give a little twirl in each of them, much to Rim's delight. The shirts were simple, conservative, wrap styles, meant to compliment the skirts, but not take attention away from the decorations. Cassidy had been worried about shoes, but Rim ensured her that no one wore shoes in the gathering hall. The dirt floor was soft enough.

After Rim made sure they had lunch (no one knows meal times better than a growing child) Margaretta returned with another woman she introduced as Phia. Phia wrapped Cassidy's red hair up and back from her face in large curls, and pinned more dried flowers into her tresses. It had been a long time since Cassidy had been so dressed up, and she was starting to catch the excitement of it.

While doing her hair, Phia and Cassidy exchanged some simple small talk, mostly Phia talking about the happy couple who were to be paired this evening, and how it was going to be Margaretta's first ceremony, so that's why she wasn't doing Cassidy's hair, and how Phia hoped she would be partnered soon, but she had only just started courting someone before the base arrived and now he works on the base and their courtship will have to wait.

Listening to Phia, part of Cassidy remembered why she rarely went to the hairdresser, but at the same time, knew she was learning a lot about the community. This was, after all, a culture of storytellers, and wasn't gossip just another way to tell some of the newest stories?

By evening, Cassidy was ready for the ceremony. Margaretta had been around again to give her some basic tips as to what to expect, though Phia had covered many of them during their time together. Cassidy would stand with both Phia, Rim, and the child's mother, and between the two of them, they would lead her through whatever she needed.

"The most important thing," Margaretta had said, "is to celebrate the couple and to enjoy yourself!"

To Cassidy, it sounded much like any wedding she

had ever attended at home.

***

After being primped and prepared for the ceremony, Cassidy was left alone while Rim and Phia went to get ready themselves. She sat outside on a bench near the village green, and just watched people wandering around, getting ready for the event. After a few minutes, Carlson came and sat next to Cassidy. He sat silently, and joined her in watching the activity.

After a little while, he started to speak.

"My father wasn't the first to visit your world. We've known about the door for almost as long as we've lived here. There are stories of our people passing through, and your people coming here. You are the first one with a shared language though. How does that work?"

"When I was on another world," Cassidy started.

Carlson cut her off. "That's not what I mean. Not the story, but what do you hear?"

"I hear you speaking in my language."

"And I hear you in mine." he said.

"I will admit though, sometimes some of the sayings are a little garbled. I think the translation is trying to make it as close to something I would recognize, but they're often not quite right."

"I can understand. Even people on the base or at the capital say we have some strange language. But it has been incorporated into our stories, so we keep using older language. Many lose it when they go to the capital, it makes them stand out, but they find it again if they come back home."

The conversation ebbed and Cassidy wondered if there was something else Carlson wanted to talk about. After a few minutes of sitting in silence, he spoke again.

"Sometimes I wish my father had never visited your world. Never discovered aeroplanes. Once he saw them, he couldn't get them out of his mind."

Cassidy looked at the man for a moment, then replied, "I have heard pilots say the same thing. Flying becomes a part of them." She thought to herself, *Like travelling to distant worlds has become part of me.* This world was making her pensive, and she wasn't certain she liked that.

"Yes," he said, "I don't understand, but I think I understand. I am a storyteller, it is part of my identity as a person. My father did not really care about stories, but when he first saw an aeroplane it was all he could talk about. He kept pushing himself to stay longer and longer, to learn more. He never got to fly one, but he did get to see them fly and saw them up close. I don't know what they must have thought, this man who would come out of the forest and talk to them in a funny language."

"We do have many languages in our world, so they may have just thought he came from another country, or was one of the land's first people, who also speak a different language from those who owned the airstrip. Although that was likely changing when your father was visiting the area."

"More than one language. Well, that is interesting. And explains some things," Carlson mused. "I could never go through the door and see the aeroplanes. By the time I was old enough, the air was too thick, too heavy. I could only be there a couple of minutes, not long enough to find the aeroplanes."

"They might have been gone. They were only there for a handful of years before they built a bigger airport much further away."

"So even if I could have made it out of the forest, I might not have seen them?"

"Possibly not, depending on when you went. That area has changed a lot in the past century, from farm land, to a railway passing nearby, to an airstrip, and now it is all houses, packed together, and a highway."

"I don't know the word highway."

Cassidy explained, "A road for cars, trucks, and other vehicles to drive a little faster to get to destinations a little further off."

"So for quicker transport?"

"In theory. But that's harder to explain."

"I see." Carlson looked at her. "My father went through the door at the wrong time. He brought your aeroplanes to our land. No. He brought the idea of aeroplanes to our land. He couldn't make them work himself, so he went to the capital where others made it work. And he still never got to fly in one. He died before they finished building the first one."

Carlson stopped, and Cassidy sat quietly, waiting for him to continue.

"If he had never gone through the door and had never seen the aeroplanes, the base wouldn't be here now. We would never have told anyone about the forest people because we never had. Even the people who moved to the capital. If they did tell people, no one listened or cared about island stories. But my father told them about aeroplanes. People from the capital came and went through the door. They even tried to create things to help them stay on the other side longer, but thankfully nothing worked. When the war started, they set up the base. They say it's because we are on the great water and the closest land to one of our enemies, but we all know it's because of the door. They want to make sure, even if they can't pass through, that no one else can. I don't know what will happen when the season starts and people start coming out of the forest. There have been more and more every year.

"Will we be able to understand them now?" he asked.

"No," she replied. "As far as I know, I am the only person in my world who can now understand everyone everywhere."

"That is probably for the best. The base would want to get information from them. Maybe make them bring back information. They may ask you to do that. Please don't. They shouldn't be here. They have taken some of our land that held important resources, they monitor what we do, and they are stealing away our young people with ideas of a modern world. When this war ends, if they ever leave, they will take many young people with them. The young people will leave the village and go to the capital and they may never come back. They will forget the stories and forget who they are.

"Thank you for letting an old man speak. This place is important to me, and I want to impress on you how important. I want to make sure that it stays safe and that you won't do anything to jeopardize our traditions."

Cassidy looked at Carlson and said, her tone as grave

as his was sad, "I won't. You have a beautiful place here, and I wouldn't want to harm it."

Carlson took her hand in his.

"Thank you."

With that, he let go of her hand, got up, and walked away, leaving her to think about what he'd said. This village was so focused on stories and tradition; would modern intervention really be so bad? Cassidy thought of all of the new technologies she had seen in her lifetime, and how exciting future technologies could be. She had seen glimpses of it on other adventures, and hoped for some of the same things at home. Why wouldn't people want these new things? She could never live a quiet life like this one. She knew, deep inside of her, she would be one of those who would leave for the capital, whatever that might bring. Stories were all well and good, and as an archaeologist she had done enough anthropology courses to know how important they were to culture and that they were how some cultures maintained their histories, but she couldn't imagine being so buried in tradition that you couldn't really explore the world. When she had discovered that a lot of archaeology was research, history books, and sitting in laboratories, she was heartbroken. At least Gamgee had given her a way out of the boring stuff.

***

The ceremony started about an hour before dusk. The hearth in the centre of the room had been covered over, and the happy couple stood on the platform, elevated for everyone to see. The townspeople formed a large circle a few steps back from the couple. Close enough to see and hear, but not so close that they were crowded.

Margaretta approached the couple. She looked regal in a dress that hung from her shoulders straight to the ground. Beads formed patterns across her chest and down the dress, creating the illusion of shape on the simple robe. The patterns looked to be symbols, but their significance was not obvious to Cassidy. Margaretta spoke quietly to the couple for a minute. In the meantime, Gertrand approached and laid a small statue in between the couple. The statue itself was of an intertwined couple, well, more of the suggestion of two people in an embrace. It was crudely done, and at the same time, worn smooth with sheen that showed it was not only old, but often touched. The statue was white, like polished quartz, but with an underlying dark colour where it was worn, suggesting a darker stone at the core.

Gertrand stepped back. Margaretta looked toward her, a slight look of panic, but Gertrand nodded, offering support, but still staying within Margaretta's line of sight. Margaretta took a deep breath and turned back to the couple.

"Sim and Darta," Margaretta spoke to the couple, but raised her voice so it carried around the room. "You have come here to pledge yourselves to one another and to be partnered. It is a happy time when two people decide that they will devote themselves to one another, and you make the pledge to be loyal and faithful to each other, to keep each other safe, and to support each other in your daily community life."

The happy couple beamed at one another.

Margaretta continued, "I ask you, in front of the community, do you pledge to be partners?"

Darta and Sim enthusiastically agreed, smiling broadly.

"Do you have your charms, given to you as children?" Margaretta asked.

The couple each produced a small sliver of black stone tied to necklaces from the folds of their shirts and passed them to Margaretta. Margaretta untied the stones from their strings.

"These were given to you on the day of your naming; they show the devotion each of your parents had for you and your love for your parents."

She picked up the idol, turning it around so that the embracing couple were no longer in view, showing a fissure where the milky white stone was rubbed or broken away, revealing the dark mineral at the centre of the statue. Margaretta took the two fragments she had just been given, and brought them to the opening. She held one piece in either hand, but as she brought them closer to the statue, she brought her hands together.

No, Cassidy thought, *they are being* pulled *together.*

Looking closer, Margaretta was trying to keep the pieces apart, but as they neared the idol, she had more and more trouble keeping her hands apart. When she got within inches of the opening, the two pieces joined together and fused. Cassidy had never seen anything like it. There were definite magnetic properties to whatever was in that statue.

Margaretta brought the now single piece of material back to the couple.

"Please cup your hands together," she directed, and

the couple did, one nestling their hands in the other's.

"Your naming charms are now one, bringing you together as one. Keep it, and each other, close to your hearts." Margaretta turned back to the crowd, "Please, let us together celebrate the partnering of Sim and Darta!"

The townspeople cheered, hugged one another, and started moving toward the couple to embrace them. Even Cassidy ended up hugged by more than just Rim and Phia. While everyone was greeting the new couple, the platform was removed and a fire lit, filling the dusk with light and warmth.

Cassidy was pleased to have been invited to the ceremony. Being invited to view another culture's major ceremonies was no small privilege, and Cassidy was more than aware of how much trust they were putting in her. At the same time, she was here on a quest, and it was to retrieve a mineral with magnetic properties. It was not on the base, but rather here, and used for marriage ceremonies. If she could hazard a guess, given that Darta and Sim had pieces from when they were infants, their piece was likely split and given to their children, should they have any. It was obviously a very important part of their culture, but Cassidy might have to figure out how to take it back for Gamgee.

The evening went on. Copious amounts of food came out, laid on small tables around the room, and a group started playing music. Everyone ate and danced and laughed and celebrated. Cassidy joined in as best she could, but kept finding herself distracted by the idol.

CHAPTER SIX

The following morning, Cassidy found Margaretta at the breakfast table. After some small talk, and talk about the ceremony, Cassidy decided to just dive in and ask about the statue.

"So, at the ceremony last night," Cassidy started, "the statue, where did it come from?"

"That is the life idol. It was old when my great-grandfather was young. It isn't part of the first stories, but is part of the earliest stories," replied Margaretta.

"Oh," Cassidy thought about how important such a piece would be to a culture, but continued, "But where did it come from?"

"We don't know," Margaretta's tone changed, becoming the more lyrical tones of someone telling a familiar story. "Ishaul, many generations before, entered the forest on a clear and warm day. He carried a bow and a knife, and wanted to bring home a feast for the high sun celebration. This was Ishaul's first hunt on his own, and with pride, he bid his partner goodbye and ventured forth. Ishaul walked many miles, following the sun, the wind, and the river. On the bank of the river, Ishaul rested. At the waterfall, Ishaul refilled his water skins. Through the rocks he climbed, and saw a beast. It was large and would make a wonderful feast. Ishaul readied his bow and let an arrow fly. The arrow struck true, at the heart of the beast, but rather than fell the beast, it bounced off, landing in the grass. The beast did not notice Ishaul's arrow, and continued to rest. Ishaul tried again. The arrow flew true, and hit the heart of the beast, only to bounce off and join its brother in the grass. Ishaul had a single arrow left. He nocked the arrow, but just as he released it, a crack of thunder overhead startled him, and the arrow went wide. The clouds closed in, and moments later, opened and rained down on Ishaul and the beast. The beast awoke, and Ishaul ran, afraid of a creature that could not be felled by arrows.

"Ishaul hid from the beast and the rain by pressing himself in the shelter of a wall of rock. In the darkness, he found a bright and shining stone. In the darkness, it glowed. With no arrows and nothing for the feast, Ishaul took back the large stone. He used a chisel, and carved the milky surface of the stone. He carved a couple, in honour of his love for his partner. The statue was a gift to her, and she cherished it. When they were blessed with a child, and the child grew, the child knocked the carving from its place above the hearth and broke through the white stone, leaving the loving couple undamaged. The child tried to repair the damage by pushing the dark flakes of stone from the inside back into the statue. Ishaul caught the child.

"'I am sorry father,' the child cried, 'but I am fixing my mistake. See, the rocks fix themselves.'

"Ishaul observed, and as the child brought a sliver of black rock to the opening at the back, it healed itself, becoming one with the statue once again. As the child went to pick up the last piece, Ishaul stepped in.

"'No,' he said, 'this last piece is for you. This statue shows the love between myself and your mother, but you are part of that love, and you should carry this stone to know that you come from our love.'

"The child took the stone, tied it with string, and wore it. When the child was grown, he asked for a second sliver for the woman he loved. Ishaul gave it freely. When they partnered, they joined their pieces together to form one. When they had a child of their own, they asked for a sliver for thc child. Ishaul gave it freely.

"Before Ishaul died, he gave the statue to his child, to celebrate their love. When Ishaul's child died, his partner returned his sliver of rock back to the statue, where it returned.

"Now we give children a piece of the statue on their name day, as a symbol of their parent's love. Those pieces are joined when they are partnered, and returned to the statue upon their death. It shows us all that we are all loved and all part of the one community."

Margaretta paused, and looked around at the other townspeople who had stopped to listen to the story.

"We have lost pieces over the years, as people have left, but it is so that they may always carry a part of the island with them, and know, no matter where they are, they are always part of us, and they are always loved. This was important yesterday, and important tomorrow, and we must remember this, even with the capital's military on our island."

Margaretta took a drink from her mug. The listening villagers seemed to know that the story was over and returned to their conversation. Cassidy did hear a few mentions of the base and the war in those discussions.

"That last part is new," explained Margaretta. "Stories are not really supposed to change, but when we talk about the morals or reasons for certain stories, we are supposed to try to reflect the current facts of life. The base is a sore spot for many, as you saw yesterday with my grandfather. But people have always left, the base is just making it easier for some."

"That was a wonderful story," said Cassidy. "It still doesn't really say where the statue came from though."

"No," replied Margaretta, "It does not, but it does give hints. Since Ishaul brought it back, people have looked for other pieces, but could not find them. We are not on a very big island, but it seems like Ishaul may have found the only piece. Why are you so interested?"

"Well, I am supposed to look for a mineral with strange magnetic properties, and it seems like your statue might be it."

"I hope not," said Margaretta, a little cautiously. "This statue has been part of our ceremonies for generations. We could possibly part with a sliver, like we give children on name day, but no more. Even that would have to be cleared by the storytellers, and they may not like the idea of more of the statue leaving than has already gone. They seem to like you enough, but they don't trust you."

Cassidy ran her hand through her hair as she thought about it. Gamgee had asked for a fairly large piece, almost half of what was in the statue. A sliver wouldn't be enough, but what if that was all she could get? There was still the matter of the inaccurate compass. There might still be something on the base, and that might be what she needed. Whatever this mineral was, it certainly seemed to have magnetic properties, but not enough to affect the compass like the base.

"I can wait. It might not even be what I'm looking for," Cassidy replied. "What I want might still be on the base; at least that's what my compass suggests."

Margaretta nodded.

"I hope it is. It would be better for you to earn a shard instead. The storytellers would much prefer that."

"But," Cassidy asked, "if the first piece is given at birth, how do the people here earn theirs?"

"No, no, not at birth," explained Margaretta. "It is given at their name day, which is usually when a child is old enough to start walking. Yes, we all get a piece just for being born here, but we do get people who come and stay on the island. We're not that isolated that there is no population movement. We don't like to see people move away, but we also welcome new people. Those people do have to spend time here and decide that it is the right place for them. Then they go through the name day ceremony, and if they want, pick a new name. Most don't, and we accept that."

"Oh, so like a citizenship ceremony? We have those in my world when people move from country to county."

Margaretta clapped, "Yes! Much like that. It's a way of saying that this is your home, where you take your tea."

"Well, that wouldn't work for me, I do have to return

to my side of the portal," Cassidy said solemnly.

"I understand that, but I trust you, and that's why I think the storytellers might let you have your own piece."

"Well, let's not worry about that until after I visit the base." Cassidy hoped she wouldn't have to wait for a naming ceremony or anything similar, but also hoped that what she needed was on the base and could be gotten without worrying about disrupting any of the island culture.

***

After breakfast, Margaretta took Cassidy to the gathering place where the wedding had taken place. In a small shrine sat the statue. Margaretta picked it up and brought it over to Cassidy. Cassidy reached toward it, then looked to Margaretta, who nodded. The statue was cool to the touch and worn smooth. Looking in the harder to touch areas, Cassidy could still see chisel marks around where the arms of the couple embraced. Other parts were significantly less defined, especially around the faces of the loving couple. Looking close, she could see how the quartz-like material was worn thin in certain areas and the darker material was starting to show through. Perhaps in another few generations it would be worn away entirely.

Cassidy took out her compass. Up close, the compass pointed directly at the statue. Cassidy pulled it back a few inches, and the needle started to waver. She took a few steps back, and it returned to bouncing between the two points.

"Your compass, right? What is it doing?" Margaretta asked.

"Something strange. Like I explained, on my world, it would point to the North Pole and I can use it to navigate. Here it keeps wavering between two points, so it wouldn't be easy to use if I were lost in the woods."

"Ah, yes, before yesterday, I had never seen one up close. We use the stars and the sun and the moss on the trees and the flow of the water," Margaretta explained. "They use other things on the base, but we use nature."

"I can understand that. I have used all of those things as well, especially this one time when I was out with just one other archaeologist and I lost my compass in a swamp and he dropped his on a rock, breaking it. That was an interesting day, but we made it out." Cassidy drifted off a little, thinking about that day out exploring with Jameson just a month ago. He threatened to never go off into the woods alone with her again. He didn't follow through, but did make a point of carrying a spare compass in a hard case after that day.

Cassidy shook off her memories and returned to the compass and the statue. After moving the compass forward and back a few more times she asked, "How does it cleave?"

Margaretta turned the statue over to the hole in the back. Cassidy could see that the white rock was thicker around the hole, likely not rubbed as much as on the carved side.

"It doesn't take much to remove a piece. It wants to be together, but at the same time, it seems to push away from itself when it is whole."

Margaretta took a small knife from a fold in her skirt and dug it into the hole. With just a little effort, she brought the knife out with a sliver of the dark stone.

"I will have to put this back. I really shouldn't have taken any out in the first place," she explained.

"I understand. I just want to look and then I will give it back," Cassidy promised.

She looked at the dark material. It was rather smooth, and shiny where it had been removed. Looking closely, she couldn't make out any grains in the rock; it reminded her of a fine-grain chert. She took a few steps back and held the compass out to the fragment. It pointed to it when right next to it, but at even an inch away it ignored the fragment and went back to the other two points. Cassidy walked back to the statue. If the compass was right next to the fragment, it would point to it, but when she brought them both to the statue, the compass pointed to the statue. On a whim, she took the outer casing off of the compass and placed the fragment on the north needle. Suddenly, the compass ignored the statue, and pointed just to the base.

"Wow, I didn't expect that," she breathed.

"Didn't expect what?" Margaretta asked.

"The material is magnetic, and will attract the compass needle. The larger the piece, the more the needle is attracted to it. But that happens for anything metallic. If I held the compass too close to my belt buckle or laid it on the hood of a car, it would throw off the reading."

"Okay..." Margaretta was clearly confused.

"But, if I put the fragment on the compass, it ignores the other points. I can bring it up to the statue and it still points just to the base."

She took a few steps back.

"And from here, it was pointing to the base and what I'm guessing is the northern pole, but with the fragment on it, it just points to the base. It must cancel out the other interference."

Cassidy wondered again if this was the material she needed to bring back. If Margaretta was this protective over a small piece, there's no way she'd be able to bring back even a significant amount without stealing it. Hopefully it wasn't what was needed and what Gamgee wanted was really on the base.

Reluctantly, she removed the piece of the statue from the compass and passed it back to Margaretta. Margaretta took it and brought it back to the statue. As she brought it inside the opening, it seemed to jump from her hand and blend back into the statue. Cassidy peered at it.

"May I?" she asked.

Margaretta nodded and Cassidy reached her hand in. The fragment wasn't just stuck back in, but had reformed back into the original material with no trace that it had ever been removed.

"This is amazing," she whispered.

"Yes, it is why we use it in our ceremonies. While there is so much in the world based in science, this feels like it is outside of that. I am sure it could be explained, but the mystery is a better story. Don't think that we worship it or anything, but it has been a part of our culture for so long that it feels almost mystical."

Margaretta beamed as she put the statue back.

"We navigate with the stars. We look for cues to read the weather. But we also rotate our crops to get the best yield and to make sure the soils stay healthy. We share stories and carry them with us. It is all part of who we are, as is this statue."

She closed the door.

"Now, I have sent word to the base; we should get you on your way," she smiled.

***

Rim led Cassidy to the edge of the village.

"If you follow the road, it will take you to the base. We never had a road here, but the base built it so they could drive their trucks back and forth to the village when they want things," explained Rim.

Cassidy thanked the child, and started along the road. She could see the fence that surrounded the base. It looked much like the older military bases she had seen in her own world; pictures of those from the Second World War. The metal fence was sturdy, but at the same time could be seen through, and she knew she wouldn't be sneaking up on anyone. Not that she wanted to. It seemed like in this world it was better to be forthcoming, if Margaretta and her fellow storytellers were any indication, and that would suit Cassidy just fine. As she came closer to the fence, she could see buildings. It looked like another village, only a short walk from the first, but could have, at the same time, been from different worlds. Margaretta's village had cozy wooden homes, all built a little differently, all with individual character; the base had rows of buildings with multiple doors, like a motel. Each section of each building, in fact each of these buildings, as there were a half dozen of them, all looked exactly the same. There weren't even any distinguishing decorations. Every window had the same curtains, and outside each door, under the window, was a small metal bench. The only difference between each room was the identifying number on the door. As she kept on, she came to larger buildings. These again were very similarly built with what looked like corrugated metal. They were all painted white, and again, hard to distinguish. She could see names painted above some of the doors, or at least what she could assume to be names. She would have to remember the general shape of the signs and hope to match them to their function. . There were some benches outside of some, and Cassidy took those to be the more social buildings, like the mess or a theatre, and guessed the ones without benches had work and maintenance functions.

Beyond the buildings, away from the road and away from the fence, stood the only building that looked different from the rest. It almost looked like a church. It was rectangular and had a spire in the centre. Cassidy squinted at the building. No, not a spire, a tower. It must be the main airfield building and the control tower. They would have to have a high vantage point to be able to see the aircraft.

At that thought, Cassidy noticed a plane taxiing down the runway that seemed to run from the main office along the backside of the residential area. She caught the movement, and still found it strange that the planes made very little noise, especially for propeller planes. She thought back to her flight to Fredericton and how her ears rang for hours after sitting so close to the engines. To be fair, it was a small plane, so everyone was pretty close to the engines. What a joy it would be to fly on a silent plane. Thinking about it, how much money had her world spent on trying to create silent aircraft? Something like this would certainly be in high demand back home.

"Perhaps the magnetic mineral had something to do with silent flight," Cassidy mused quietly.

She continued on toward the base. As she approached the gate, she noticed more activity inside. Most of it seemed to be soldiers running the perimeter of the fence, but others who were just milling around seemed to notice her back. Perhaps she should have asked Margaretta for some clothes, instead of wearing jeans and a button shirt. She certainly didn't look like one of the locals in this outfit, with the women mostly in long skirts.

The people of the base also offered a level of contrast in comparison to the village. The townspeople all wore locally made clothing. Some of the fabric seemed to be machine-made, but many also wore hand-woven cloths. Almost everything was hand-sewn. As she got closer, Cassidy noted that the soldiers all had identical uniforms, and they looked, by her standards, relatively modern. They didn't look like the coarser fabrics of 19th century wars, but the smooth lines of machine-made fabrics.

It was interesting to think that there seemed to be a modern world so very close to the island, but somehow this village kept its traditions, even if that might mean more work. Cassidy had participated in archaeological workshops to give better understanding of how fabrics were made and the traditional tools used, and she couldn't imagine going through the effort if ready-made fabrics were available. Sure, she could understand it from a cultural point of view, and did treasure the hand-woven skirt that she saved for important occasions, and loved her knit hat for the cold weather, but could not understand the want to continue such labour-intensive activities except as a hobby.

She decided to ask Margaretta about the tradition. There was obviously contact to the ominous capital, and people did seem to flow back and forth, but faced with a modern world, they must actively hold on to the traditional ways. From an anthropological point of view, it was fascinating. Not that Cassidy would write a paper on it, but she knew colleagues who would love such a research opportunity. For one, she couldn't publicize the presence of the portals, and second, it's not like she'd really take the time to sit and write a paper to put out for peer-review.

Nearing the gate, the two soldiers on duty stopped her.

"You don't look like you're from the village," one said suspiciously.

"That's just rude," scolded the other. "But he's right, you don't look like you're from the village. Or from anywhere else for that matter. That's a strange outfit."

Cassidy gave them each a quick look. Both were younger than her, with a little of the slouch of youth in their demeanour. Trying to stand at attention seemed like a lot of work, especially for the first one who spoke. His stance seemed better suited for milling around a shopping mall instead of guarding a military base. The other was a little more poised, but not by much. Both wore crisp uniforms, clean, bright boots, and small hats that just barely covered their heads. Other than the hats, which had no rims to keep the sun out of their eyes, but rather seemed to be designed to just cover the tops of their heads and hide their hair, the uniforms were very similar to those Cassidy might have seen on any base. The attitude was more like what she would have seen from teenage cadets when they didn't think supervisors were looking.

"I was told my visit was arranged. My name is Cassidy Cane and Margaretta, one of the storytellers from the village, sent me," Cassidy stated, trying to sound authoritative.

"I don't know nothing about that," said the first soldier.

"Oh, knock it off, tough guy." The second soldier turned to Cassidy. "Yeah, we were told someone from the village but not from the village was coming. Hang on, I'll go call it in."

The second soldier walked away, leaving Cassidy to suffer the glares of the first one.

He must be new to this, she thought.

The first soldier reappeared.

"I'll escort you in. Seems like the director of flight has been waiting for you. I wouldn't want to keep her waiting any longer."

Wonderful, thought Cassidy. *I took my time and enjoyed the walk and have kept this director of flight waiting. No one told me I should have rushed. Oh well, let's hope it doesn't ruin her first impression.*

CHAPTER SEVEN

The soldier was silent during their walk to the large building with the control tower. This didn't really help Cassidy, who was becoming a little more nervous with every step. She thought she might have preferred the glares and snarky remarks from the other one at the gate, instead of the professional silence as soldiers continued to run exercises around them.

Once in the building, the soldier had to buzz an intercom.

"Private Seware with Cassidy Cane to see Director Spear," he called in clipped tones.

Director Spear, Cassidy thought glumly, *that name does not sound like someone who tolerates tardiness.*

The intercom crackled with something indistinguishable, and a click followed by a buzz indicated the door was unlocked. Cassidy's escort opened it and directed her through. The inside of the building was sterile, almost hospital-like, with clean, white walls, long corridors dotted with white doors, and no decorations to be seen.

The soldier led Cassidy through a hallway, turned a corner, down another hall, up a flight of stairs, down another hall, and up another two flights of stairs, down yet another hallway, around a corner, and stopped at a door.

"This is Director Spear's office. Knock and she will let you in," Seware said, before turning and walking away.

I hope I'll be able to find my way out, thought Cassidy as she turned and knocked on the door.

"Enter," said a female voice.

Cassidy did as bade, summoned her courage, and stepped through the door.

As she entered, a woman a little older than herself stood up from her desk and walked toward Cassidy. Her uniform was similar in cut to the two soldiers at the gate, but a little more polished. She wore the green pants and shirt professionally, but also gave a feeling of being comfortable in the uniform. Unlike most of the soldiers Cassidy had seen so far, Director Spear's head was uncovered, and her auburn hair was back in a tight braid. She came around the desk and extended a hand to Cassidy. Cassidy shook it. The director's handshake was firm, but Cassidy no longer felt intimidated by her surroundings.

"Good morning, my name is Sharisan Spear. I am the Director of Flight here at the Vering Island Airbase. You must be Cassidy Cane," stated Director Spear.

"Cassidy is fine; thank you for seeing me."

"Then you can call me Shari. Really, I only expect Director Spear from those who serve under me."

"You know," mused Cassidy, "I have been here two days, and this is the first time I have heard the name of this place. In the village they just call it the village, the town, or 'this place'. It is sort of nice to know the name of the island."

Shari laughed. "I have noticed that as well. It is a strange place, this island. I am from Docknew, on the coast of the mainland of Astrada. It is nowhere near the capital city of Tian, but to most of the islanders here, it might as well all be one place. Except, of course, those who spent some time on the mainland; they have a better understanding of the size of the country. But I digress, let's have a seat and talk. Would you like something to drink?"

Cassidy answered affirmatively, and Shari poured two mugs of warm, golden liquid. It was fruity and spicy, not unlike a mulled cider Cassidy might have at a fall harvest festival.

"So, down to business," Shari directed. "I don't have much information, but you are from through the door in the woods."

Cassidy sputtered a little and choked on her drink.

Shari saw her anguish and tried to calm Cassidy.

"Oh, don't worry. The elders, or storytellers, sent word about you. We, of course, know about the door. That is one of the reasons we have a base here. It is not just a staging centre for aircraft, but a defence base. Your world seems to have many amazing technologies, and we cannot allow that to fall into enemy hands. We may not be able to spend much time in your world, but we can make certain no one else does either."

"I never really thought of it that way," Cassidy responded. "I have been to other worlds, but often no one knows about the portals. It's like it's an open secret here."

"Well, it sort of is. Of course, the general population doesn't know anything about it. Heck, most of the soldiers here don't know that is one of our missions. To most of the world, aeroplanes are our own invention, not something that was taken from another world and adapted to our own."

"I am curious about that. Planes at home are loud and the fuel makes them rather smelly, but yours are quiet and seem to have no environmental impact on the air."

Shari considered this statement before answering.

"Well, we did have to change quite a lot. Frake, the one who brought us back the plans, couldn't figure out how to change the design for use here; that's why he brought it to Tian, to get the help he needed. We couldn't make the aeroplane exactly the same as what is in your world because it would dirty our air. That is why we can no longer use the door, your air is so heavy that we cannot breathe there. Frake, years ago, could only stay for a few hours at a time. According to the storytellers, people moved more freely between worlds, but that was many years and many generations ago."

"Yeah, over the past couple of centuries our technologies have changed drastically, with a reliance on coal then fossil fuels that have changed how we live, but also pollute the world."

"Pollute. Fossil fuel," mused Shari. "Those aren't really words that we have here. We took what Frake gave us and looked for other ways to power it."

"What did you use?" Cassidy really hoped it might be the mineral she was looking for.

"Oh, now, I can't share all of our secrets," Shari smirked a little. "We do use halfstone, which is our main power source, from aeroplanes to lights and everything else. I know aeroplanes came from your world, but I still can't share how we've changed them. Not unless you can share information with us, then my superiors might be more willing to tell you."

Cassidy hesitated. "No, I really don't have anything I could easily share. I don't really know that much about modern technology. I study the past, so most of the technologies I've studied are hundreds, if not thousands of years old."

"That's too bad. But if you are not interested in technology, why do you ask about ours?"

"Two reasons. First, flying on planes at home can be very loud. I flew on one to get to the portal, one that looked a lot like the ones you have with the propellers, and it was so loud that my ears were ringing for hours after. At least the jet engines are much more comfortable. The second reason—"

"One moment, aeroplanes are different in your world?"

Oops, thought Cassidy, *perhaps I need to better watch what I say about technology.*

"Some of them are. They changed since they were first invented." Cassidy paused to try to figure out how to respond. "You see, the earlier planes used propellers, and from what I saw about the airfield that Frake visited, it would have been small prop planes used for a few years. Since then, technology has changed to make planes faster. I have no idea how a jet engine works, just that they can go faster and I think use a different kind of fuel, though I'm not sure about that. They also need much longer runways, so probably couldn't work on that airfield. It was probably one of the reasons why it closed"

Cassidy decided to not tell her that jet engines had greater distance capabilities, or their use in weaponry or space travel. Probably best to not give away those secrets, and if she could, give some of the disadvantages.

"Can you get us the information on how to use those jet engines?"

Yes, with a quick internet search, thought Cassidy, but instead she said, "Probably not. A lot of that technology is classified. State secrets."

"Hmmmm… that is unfortunate. That would really help us in this war," replied Shari with a tinge of disappointment in her voice. "So, what is your other reason for interest in our aeroplanes?"

"Well, you see, I am here to find a mineral with magnetic properties, and while I don't understand all of the principles of magnetism, I figure there might be a way that it could be used to power your silent planes."

"And why do you want it?" Shari was getting a little suspicious of Cassidy, and wondered if she was being entirely truthful about not being able to share information.

"You see, I work for a man who does a lot of good in the world. He sends me places to find things that he uses to help people in my world. He has cured diseases because of what he has found elsewhere. I help because he can't physically visit other worlds anymore."

"Is he sick? Why can't he cure himself?" asked Shari.

"No, just a little too old for it. He says adventure is for young people, so here I am!" Cassidy smiled, momentarily recalling some of her adventures since she met Dr. Gamgee.

"How does he know where to send you?"

Cassidy paused. "I don't know. I have sometimes wondered that myself."

"You don't ask? You are a good soldier, we look for that here."

Cassidy was a little offended at the idea of being a soldier who doesn't question. She questioned a lot, but never really where Gamgee gets his information. If she asked, she might not be sent on these missions anymore, and that would mean less adventure and more work in the lab.

"I have a job already," Cassidy replied a little curtly.

Shari laughed, "I didn't mean to offend. You just don't seem like the type who wouldn't question. I do a lot of recruiting, and your comment would have flagged you as someone I would want. Intelligent, but at the same time, not questioning."

Cassidy still didn't know what to think on the matter. She sat there in silence, thinking about her own actions. Maybe if she had questioned a little more she wouldn't have ended up in some of the more dangerous situations. But then, weren't those situations the ones that made it all worthwhile?

"So I have offended. Okay, let's go back to your question. I will tell you that there is nothing magnetic that fuels our aeroplanes. We do use some magnetic devices for navigation, but not to make the aircraft fly."

Cassidy perked up a little, "Could I maybe see some of the navigational equipment?"

"I don't see why not. It is not a state secret. In fact, it is technology that is so readily available that we give it to kids when they want to go exploring."

That sounded familiar to Cassidy. She reached into her pocket and pulled out her compass. She opened it up and showed it to Shari.

"Is it something like this? Like a pocket compass?" Cassidy asked.

Shari looked at the compass. "Yes, exactly like that. We usually call it nav for navigation."

Cassidy looked down at the compass. It was still wavering between two points, but this time it seemed to be one beyond the base, and off to the side. If the source of the magnetism was at the base, then likely the compass would have been even more erratic, or very still and pointing directly to the source. Cassidy wasn't sure what would happen, but that it would indicate something different.

"I see you get the same interference on yours as we do on ours," Shari observed. "There is something on this island that throws off our instruments. We have to be at least a hundred miles out into the ocean before the navs level out and just point toward the pole."

"From the village, it would point to the base, so that's why I assumed something was here," Cassidy explained.

"Yes, we are on the line to the pole from the village."

So the equivalent to north or south, thought Cassidy. *Then what is the other thing?*

"We have tried to find the source of the interference," Shari continued, "but without any success. We have flown over, but the source seems both large and small at the same time. We have narrowed down a potential area, but even on the ground we cannot find it. Unfortunately, we have lost aeroplanes when they have tried to land here and lost their way."

"That's tragic," Cassidy replied, then added, without thinking, "but easily fixed."

She stopped when she realized what she had said. That wasn't information for her to give. She had reacted to the idea of lives being lost, not what it would mean to Margaretta and her kin.

"You know how to fix the problem?" Shari asked with interest.

"Well, it's not really mine to tell." Cassidy hesitated, "It belongs to the people of Vering."

Shari stood up and leaned toward Cassidy, both hands on her desk.

"We have lost many men and women because of this anomaly. You must tell me how to fix this navigational problem. Lives are at stake," Shari insisted.

Cassidy thought, and spoke carefully, "There is something at the village, but I really cannot say more. It is important to the people there."

"Important enough that they would allow people to die for it?" Shari started to raise her voice. "Important enough that they would risk losing the war?"

Cassidy stood up. She did not appreciate being spoken to in such a way. She was not one of Shari's soldiers.

"Have you met the people in that village? Sure, many serve here, but many more would happily see the war over if it meant this base was gone. Taking the statue would give them even more reason to resent the base, and relations would get even worse," Cassidy argued.

"Statue?"

Cassidy mentally cursed and thought, *My big mouth. I*

need to learn to think before I speak.

"Statue," repeated Shari. "That trinket I have heard they use in ceremonies? We have to fight with soldiers from the village to take off those necklaces that are all part of this statue."

That gave Cassidy an idea.

"Would the soldiers give up their necklaces for the war effort? The mineral in those can fix the compass issue, and they should have plenty for the base to use." Then Cassidy added hopefully, "Then you could leave the statue be."

"That could work, depending on how much we have on base, and how much we need to use. But we have hundreds of planes. No, we need the source. What if it falls into enemy hands?"

"That's asinine!" exclaimed Cassidy. "You know full-well it won't fall into enemy hands because the whole point in the base being here is to protect the portal. You said so yourself!"

Shari gave Cassidy a serious look.

"Watch yourself. I could arrest you where you stand. This is a military base after all, and I have to put the safety of my troops first. I might feel you are keeping important information from us, and could hold you until I feel you have given me all the information I need."

Cassidy stepped back.

"Please, let me talk to the storytellers at the village and explain the situation. I'm sure they'll be agreeable to help you. If you just take it, you'll ruin whatever goodwill they have."

"Why am I worried about their goodwill when lives

are on the line?" Shari asked.

"What is the point in fighting a war if it only hurts your fellow countrymen?" Cassidy countered.

Shari considered.

"Fine." Shari sat, rested her elbows on the desk and tented her fingers. "Go, talk to the village. Talk to the elders. I will collect what I can on base. Tomorrow morning I expect them to provide enough to fix all of our navigational equipment. I do not do this lightly. If they have something to save lives and help win the war, then we will have it. Make sure you convince them."

"I will do what I can to keep the peace."

"I am not as worried about the peace as I am about winning this war," Shari said, deadly serious.

CHAPTER EIGHT

Cassidy found herself walking back to the village. She was feeling lost, and angry at herself. Once again, she didn't stop to think before she spoke and she may have messed things up. On one side, if Shari could use the stone to save lives, that was a good thing. But on the other side, this statue has been important to the people of the village for generations. They already felt like the base had ruined their way of life, and now it was going to take their sacred object from them. Well, maybe it wouldn't come to that. After all, there were a number of people on the base who had shards of the stone, so maybe there would be more than enough.

Cassidy almost laughed at herself for such a thought. She knew full-well that there were a significant number of planes flying to and from the base. There was no way the military would stop with just the aircraft doing patrols or regular milk runs. They'd want to outfit all of their aircraft with better navigational equipment on the off chance they had to turn back or get diverted to the island. At the very least, they'd want every plane that had even the slightest chance of flying near the island upgraded. Then, after the war, they'd probably want any military, diplomatic, or commercial aircraft outfitted with it. If her home was any indication, there were probably people already discussing the prospect of commercial air travel after the war. In her own history, commercial air travel over the ocean was almost non-existent prior to the Second World War, but with the improvements made during the war, air travel between North America and Europe became much safer and commercial flying became much more common once the war ended. It would be reasonable to guess something similar would happen in this world. After all, they had not really worked to improve aircraft much before this war, but were certainly making a great deal of use of it now that there was a world-wide conflict.

A horrible thought crossed Cassidy's mind. She didn't know anything about this war. Everyone was very friendly, even if Commander Shari was a little intense, but who was the aggressor in this war? If she helped, would she be helping the good guys or the bad guys? Of course they would count themselves as the good guys, so she'd never know by talking to people. If the portal had dropped her into an Axis country in 1944, no one she spoke to would think they would be considered the bad side by the history books, would they? She kind of wished she had paid more attention to modern history.

This mission was turning into more thinking and less action than she was used to. Usually it was so straight forward, and this time she was left wondering about what to do, who she might be hurting, and even who she might be helping.

At the edge of the village, Rim saw her and ran over

to greet her.

"How was the base?" Rim asked. "I never get to go see it. I want to see the aeroplanes and the soldiers. Their buildings are very different from ours, and all boring."

Cassidy laughed at the child's excitement.

"Yes, it was pretty boring. No colour there at all, not like here. And all of the buildings look exactly the same. Even inside, everything looked the same. The soldiers were okay. Some were friendly, some tried to be scary."

"Scary how? Did someone threaten you?"

"Oh no no no. They just tried to make me feel scared, but it didn't work. Most people there were very nice. Do you know where Margaretta is?" Cassidy figured if she didn't head off Rim's questions she'd never get away.

"I think she's in her home," Rim said, paused, and then gave a little jump. "I can take you there!"

Rim led the way, asking questions about the base the entire time. Cassidy knew it was just curiosity on the child's part, but also wondered if relations would be better with the base if they did things like tours for the people of the village. Rim certainly didn't see them as monsters, but, at the same time, Rim also wouldn't understand the fears over losing their culture to the "capital".

Once at the cottage, Rim barged in, announcing that Cassidy was back from the base, and started recounting some of what Cassidy had said. Margaretta listened for a few moments, then shooed Rim away, stating the need to talk to Cassidy. Margaretta invited Cassidy in, brought her to an open room, and sat her down on a cushion. Margaretta sat on another and, before she could say anything, Olisker came in with three mugs of a warm, spiced, berry drink. He handed the mugs around, and Cassidy took a moment to smell the spicy sweet drink and take in the room.

It was certainly the living area of the house. There was a small, low table in the centre of the room, and cushions all around. A nice spot for lounging or for a group of people to gather and comfortably talk. There were a couple of paintings on the wall, both landscapes, and it looked like a mixed media work as there was a sparkle and roughness to the beaches that implied sand was mixed in with the pigments. Margaretta's living room was ringed with bookcases, the paintings sitting over shorter cases. Cassidy couldn't read the script, assuming the decorative scrolling symbols just didn't translate clearly, but could guess that many of these books, especially the older-looking tomes, were probably some of the stories she helped keep, just written down. Overall, Cassidy thought the room was cozy and comfortable, and could almost see herself enjoying the space to do some reading or research. Almost.

After a moment, Margaretta started the conversation. "How did it go at the base?" she asked.

"Honestly, I'm not sure. We seemed to have a pretty good conversation, but then I seemed to just say too much a few times."

Olisker narrowed his eyes at Cassidy. "What does that mean?"

"Well," she continued, sheepishly, "I misspoke about jet engines, a newer kind of engine for planes at home. They're faster and can go further, and I shouldn't have said anything because I think the flight director might want me to bring her information on them. And that had me kind of flustered," Cassidy was rambling now, agitated and worried, "and we started talking about planes crashing because of the funny navigation around the island and I mentioned the compass and the magnetic stone, and she was interested in it and is going to experiment with what the locals on the base have and I'm worried that that's not enough and she's so focused on the war effort that now I'm afraid..."

Margaretta looked panicked, but calmed her features and put a hand on Cassidy's shoulder.

"Breathe. You are saying a lot, but it's coming out mixed up. I think you have to tell us, but just one thing at a time. Take a drink. Breathe."

Cassidy took a long drink from her cup. Her pulse raced, but not in the way she craved. This was agitated and erratic. She took another drink. Cassidy looked at the other two, her anxiety feeding theirs. She took a deep breath and started again.

"I was talking with Flight Director Spear. We were having a nice conversation, but she made me sort of flustered. She knew things I didn't expect, like that I was from the other world, and asked for things. But I should have expected that, given that planes come from my world. Next thing I know, I'm talking about jet engines, which is a newer kind of engine that can go further than the kind of planes you have now. We started talking about navigation and how this island does something strange to compasses. She said people have died because of it. And without thinking, or maybe just thinking about how people have died, I said how the piece from the statue fixed it."

Margaretta and Olisker looked horrified. Cassidy tried

to explain and apologize.

"I didn't mention the statue itself! I just said 'the piece of stone' and she figured it out. She knows a lot about this place, and my place, and I didn't expect that, but I should have expected that because isn't that what militaries are like everywhere? On every world? They always know more than you expect."

She started to panic again, and Margaretta once again put her hand on Cassidy's shoulder. Cassidy ran her hands through her hair, then picked up her cup and took another drink.

"She's going to ask the people from the village who are on the base to give her their fragments of the statue. I don't know if she's just going to ask, or if she's going to take them. And she's asked me to ask for more; enough for their planes. She thinks it's all superstition and your statue doesn't matter when people are dying."

Olisker got up. "I'm going to gather the storytellers. We will have to talk about it and figure out what we have to do."

Margaretta nodded and said, "I'll take care of Cassidy. Can you send someone to get Phia to come and sit with her? I will come when Phia arrives. Please start without me."

Olisker left and Cassidy started to calm a little.

"I have messed everything up," Cassidy sighed. "I'm used to going places where I don't have to think about things like this. It's always so clear, and then here it's all so muddled. The statue is important to you, it's been in your first stories, but it's important to the base because people are dying. I've studied situations like this in my undergrad ethics courses, but I've never had to deal with something myself. And when I find myself involved, I just ruin everything."

"Hush now," Margaretta calmed. "We will work it out. The statue is important, but, like you've said, people are dying. I did not know that. The storytellers didn't know that. We'll talk. We'll figure something out..."

Margaretta didn't sound very confident, but was steady in how she spoke, and that helped calm Cassidy. Moments later, Phia came in. Margaretta asked her to sit with Cassidy, and got up and left, repeating, "We'll figure something out."

***

A few hours later, evening was falling and Phia suggested they get something to eat. Cassidy hadn't eaten since that morning, but was nervous about facing the storytellers. Phia reassured her and they went out. The food was good, but the tension seemed high. There wasn't as much conversation as at other meals. The storytellers were at a table to themselves, with no one near them.

"When they do that, it means they are discussing something important," Phia explained, although Cassidy really didn't need the explanation. She just wished she could have some sort of an indication that things would be okay, but they were all so engrossed in their discussion that none of the storytellers even noticed her and Phia come in. Even Rim was more subdued than usual, not bouncing around, just quietly eating with another group. In fact, all of the kids seemed quiet. Everyone seemed to know something was wrong, and Cassidy wondered if they all knew that she was the one who caused it.

After they ate, Cassidy and Phia went back to Phia's home.

"If Margaretta wants us, she will check here after her own house," Phia explained.

Phia's living room was like Margaretta's in that it had a short table surrounded by cushions. Cassidy was surprised that Phia's home was not nearly as colourful, and most of the cushions were dark colours, deep purples and blacks. There weren't as many bookcases, but there were a few shelves with a few books, and a lot of knick-knacks. Cassidy took a closer look and recognized some things. There was a green glass cola bottle, some red bricks stamped with English lettering, a railroad spike, what looked to be musket balls, and a very old hafted scraper and bone needle. The scraper was a small stone tool used by the Indigenous people who used to live along the Wolastoq River, renamed the Saint John by Europeans, to prepare hides. It was wrapped in some very dry, very brittle sinew. Cassidy longed to touch it, but knew it must be at least a few hundred years old and would probably crumble if she touched it. But to find such a thing intact was any archaeologist's dream.

Phia caught her looking at the treasures.

"My family has used the door for many years. It used to be that we were the ones who would go through and see what we could find. It was one of the women of my family who found the door when out collecting plants. Margaretta would tell it better – she's the storyteller after all – but it was our family responsibility to collect things. We used to trade with people on the other side of the door, but then new people came, and the trade changed.

It became less about sharing food and more about sharing things. Then it got harder and harder to travel through the door, and my family stopped going."

Phia looked at the items, a hint of sadness in her features.

"Have you ever gone through the door?" Cassidy asked.

"I tried once, but the air was so thick and heavy that I could only stay there for a minute. It was nice to look around, though, and feel a different sun, even if it was just for a moment."

Silence weighed heavy in the room.

"It's a strange thing," Phia continued, "having a role, a responsibility, passed down through the generations, only to have it taken away through no fault of your own. It is something I've had trouble reconciling. I even left for a while, trying to find a new role, but I haven't found what is right. I more end up taking care of the people who come through the door, rather than getting to go through to meet them."

She indicated the objects around the room. "We still trade, but it isn't the same because it's whatever people have on them when they come through, and many seem to have very little, so we would rather give than trade. It's not easy for us, though. We don't have a lot here, although we could if we opened up more to the capital..."

Phia faded off again.

"What sort of things did you trade for?" Cassidy prompted.

"Interesting foods, and you do many wonderful things with different kinds of metals on your side of the door. We have traded for pots and pans, and tools to fish with. We have such things here, of course, but some of yours work differently. When your people started using nets made out of different material, and the thin line to fish with, it was so much more durable than us growing plants to make the rope to make the nets. And sometimes we could get the fire rocks, and those we could keep for long, hard winters when the dry wood gets low."

Plastic, nylon, and coal. *Interesting and practical trades,* thought Cassidy as she looked at an empty soda can.

"I don't think they fish on that river a whole lot anymore, it seems mostly like a city. And not many people use coal to heat their homes anymore." Cassidy brightened. "I will have to repay everyone's kindness, so maybe I will be able to get some of those things to bring back through. I can't promise anything, but I can try." She wondered if she would be able to talk to anyone in the homeless community about such trade, but, like Phia said, chances are they had very little to start with anyway.

"Oh," Phia brightened, "that would be wonderful! I don't suppose you live near the door, do you?"

"No. Once I leave after this, it would be difficult for me to get back."

"Well, at least it would be something. Many thanks."

"Don't thank me until I see if I can do it." Cassidy gave a little smile, worried about what was going to happen with the statue.

With that, a child younger than Rim popped into the room.

"Hello Tor," Phia introduced. "Are you here to collect Cassidy?"

The child nodded and said shyly, "The storytellers need her."

CHAPTER NINE

Cassidy quickly said goodbye to Phia and rushed after Tor. The child was nearly running and Cassidy struggled to keep up. Tor brought her to another house, a few lit lamps flickering through the window to stave off the first hints of twilight.

"They want to talk to you; I said I'd get you," Tor said quietly but proudly, and brought Cassidy to the door before running off again. Cassidy kind of wanted to run away as well.

"Come in Cassidy," came Margaretta's voice from inside.

Cassidy took a deep breath, and entered. All of the storytellers were standing around a kitchen, each holding mugs. Margaretta took a mug from the table and offered it to Cassidy. She took it and wrapped her hands around its warmth, taking comfort in the feeling and smelling the spicy liquid. She didn't take a drink, she was too nervous for that.

Sasamuel cleared his throat and started. "Cassidy." His voice was stern, but not intimidating. Cassidy relaxed just a little. "In talking to the flight director at the base, you have put us in a difficult situation. We know the idol has no magical properties and is just a symbol of a long-ago story that connects us to this place. But you are saying that if we give some of it to the flight director it could save lives. We have decided that we will give a large piece from inside of the statue to help the fighters, because that is what we do, we help." This last bit wasn't said for Cassidy, as Sasamuel shot Carlson a hard look, who in turn, muttered something about "people through the door should keep their stuff on their own side."

The rest of the storytellers, Margaretta included, glared at him. Sasamuel continued, "Not everyone is in agreement, but we have been helping the people who have come to our island for generations. Many of our stories involve helping people, so we're not going to stop now. Plus," again he glared at Carlson, "the people through the door are not the ones who gave us the aeroplanes; that was our own people going through and learning new technologies." Looking back to Cassidy, his features softened. "We help. Sometimes we'd trade with the other side of the door, but we never ask for anything. If people are dying, it is our responsibility to help. Tomorrow, we will bring some of the statue to the base, and hopefully they will let our people keep their personal fragments of the statue."

Margaretta stepped around the table and over to Cassidy. She took Cassidy's mug, still full, and laid it on the table. She took both of Cassidy's hands in her own.

"We know you didn't mean to say anything to the flight director, but in a way, we are happy that you did. We did not know that people were dying trying to get to our island. Don't despair, just, if something like this comes up again, maybe talk to us first," she said with a kind smile.

"I will. Thank you. And I am still very sorry for all of it," Cassidy replied. Margaretta looked at Cassidy once more before wrapping her arms around her and giving her a big hug.

***

Cassidy awoke the next morning to general commotion. She could hear people yelling and running around. She threw off her blanket and grabbed her bag, pulled out some clothes and hauled them on. She quickly tied her hair back and walked out the door.

Soldiers were marching past her building. She looked toward the centre of town and saw villagers running around and soldiers moving toward the gathering hall. She started moving that way, trying to find out what was happening. She found Director Spear walking out of the building holding the statue. Margaretta followed close on her heels.

"Please, don't take it," Margaretta begged. "We are happy to share it, but please, don't take the whole thing! It's important to our community."

Shari turned to face Margaretta.

"We need this. We need all of this. This will save lives. This will help win the war." She looked at the idol then back to Margaretta. "It is your duty to help your countrymen and women to help win the war." Shari turned on her heels and marched away, barking orders to her soldiers as she went.

Sasamuel came up next to Cassidy.

"She took the idol. All of it. The rest of the storytellers are not happy, and when word gets around the village that you told them about it, well," Sasamuel paused, then said, very seriously, "we're a giving people, but it might be best if you leave for a little while until things calm down somewhat."

Cassidy just looked at him for a moment and said, "I didn't mean to cause this."

"I know," he replied, "but it will take everyone else a while to know that as well."

Cassidy turned back to the guest house, threw her stuff in her bag and quickly went to the border of the village. Just past the last house, Phia and Rim caught up with her.

"Are you leaving Cassidy?" Rim asked.

"I think it's for the best right now," Cassidy replied.

"What happened? Why are the soldiers here?"

"I made a mistake and the soldiers took your idol. But I am going to go away to try to make it right." Cassidy knelt down to talk to Rim face-to-face. "I will fix this." She looked up at Phia. "I will."

Phia took Cassidy's hand and pulled her back to her feet. "We know, Cassidy. You are a good person."

Cassidy smiled, and left the village.

***

She wasn't sure what she should do. She walked into the woods and just walked for a while. She couldn't go back to the village, but she did have to try to get the idol back. She also didn't want to go back to her own world yet, not when she had found the mineral she needed, but lost it. She wandered for a while, not really knowing which way she was going, until the trees thinned and she could see the base.

If nothing else, she thought, *perhaps I could talk to someone about it.*

Cassidy approached the gate and saw the same soldiers as before. She approached Private Seware, not really looking for the aggression of the other soldier.

"Hello. I am wondering if I might be able to meet with the flight director. Please." Cassidy tried to sound confident, but her nerves were getting the better of her.

"One moment, and I will call in," replied Private Seware.

The private walked away, leaving Cassidy once again with the other soldier.

"Um, my name is Cassidy, by the way," she tried being friendly, but only received a grunt in reply.

Better than being rude like last time, Cassidy thought.

Private Seware came back. "Flight Director Spear is not available right now, but has invited you to stay here for the time being. She will find you when she is ready."

That solves that problem, thought Cassidy as she allowed herself to once again be led on base.

Private Seware brought Cassidy to a barracks and gave her a key to one of the rooms.

"You can leave your bag here. This is your room for the time being. The flight director said she might not see you today."

Cassidy opened the door to a spartan room containing a small bed, desk, and chair. She stepped in and laid her bag on the bed. Turning back to Private Seware at the door, she noted the door to a bathroom and a small wardrobe. Basic, but comfortable.

Locking the door behind her and pocketing the key, Cassidy followed Private Seware to the mess hall.

"You can move freely within the two buildings, but nowhere else on the base. Meals are available for an hour after dawn, an hour at high sun, and for two hours before dusk. When she wants you, Flight Director Spear will send for you."

With that, Private Seware turned and walked away, leaving Cassidy in the empty mess hall. Cassidy wandered outside, looking at the sun, thinking that there might be another hour or so before the sun was at its zenith, so she went back to her room and unpacked her small bag and washed herself and some of her clothes in the small sink. Not that the village was unclean, and as the only person in the guest house the bath was private, but Cassidy was a little uncomfortable with the communal space and that people didn't seem to knock at the village.

Refreshed, but still unsure of what to do, Cassidy went back to the mess hall to find food. With all of the confusion of the morning, she had not eaten, but still was not really hungry, but thought it was best to do something. She could smell the food as soon as she passed through the door, and her stomach did give a little grumble. The hall was much more active than before, with thirty or forty people in the room. Some were sitting, while others were in line, holding plates. Cassidy picked up a plate and took her place at the end of the line. Within moments, some soldiers got in line behind her.

"Hi!" one young man said to her, "you must be the one from through the door. I'm Breen, this is Aline," indicating the woman next to him, "and behind her is Trice." The other two nodded in acknowledgement.

"Does everyone know about the door?" Cassidy asked.

"At this point, just about. Half of us here are from the village; myself and Aline were born there. Trice is from a small town on the other side of the channel, so is almost from the island." Aline elbowed Trice, and he grinned at the gentle teasing. "So we've always known about the door, but news got around the base pretty quick, both from talking to our families and from the on-base rumour-mill, that there was someone from the other side who could talk to us."

Trice piped up with, "Thanks for finding out about the compass. I lost my brother a couple of months ago, and they figure he just got lost. So, thanks." Trice blushed a little, but put out his hand. Cassidy took his hand and he shook hers briefly before dropping her hand and letting his fall back to his side. Cassidy felt like she was blushing a little herself.

Before she could say anything, Cassidy found herself far enough in the line to be at a small counter. Following the person in front of her, she placed her plate on the counter, and the person behind the counter put some food on it. She pushed the plate along the counter, and other staff put more food on her plate. When it was full, she took the plate, walked toward the long tables and hesitated. Breen came up behind her.

"Drinks are over this way." He led her to a variety of

juices in jugs. They each poured up a glass, and he invited her to sit with them.

The four of them sat at the end of one of the long tables, and Cassidy started to pick at her mountain of food. Once again, she couldn't recognize anything and really wanted the comfort of something she knew. The other three asked her a few questions, but then started to talk about their own lives on the base.

"So, do you think they're going to put the new nav equipment on all the aeros? Even the little ones? Or is it just for the big ones?

"Oh, I hope it's the little ones, too. I have a supply run coming up and want to give it a try."

"Did you hear Thulu got reprimanded for trying to sneak off base? Seems he's got a bit of a thing for one of the guys in the village."

"I didn't hear that one, but it sounds like Celia might have had a secret date with Amer."

"Wait, Celia on the gate? And I hear it was Amer in the village that Thulu liked!"

"Sounds like a love triangle!"

Cassidy wasn't really listening while the three discussed base and village gossip. They all seemed friendly enough, and that 'thank you' from Trice had sent her back into her thought spiral. Meeting people who were so grateful about the discovery made her feel even more confused. And she still had to figure out how to get some of the statue back to Gamgee.

Cassidy was pulled out of her thoughts as the other three tried to engage her a little.

"So, what can you tell us about the other side of the

door?" Aline asked.

"And what are the aeros like?" Trice leaned forward, waiting for an answer.

Cassidy considered. "First, I can't tell you much about the planes. That's what we call them. Airplane, or planes for short. I have flown in them, but only as a passenger."

"A passenger? Like on a supply run?"

"Not really. We use planes for military runs, sure, but most air travel is commercial, meaning people pay to be flown from one place to another, often to go on business or holiday."

The trio were shocked. Aline wanted to know more. "So, not just supplies, but for leisure? We don't have enough for something like that!"

"We didn't either, at first, but after our last worldwide war people started using planes instead of boats to get around the world."

It was Breen's turn to question. "You had a whole world war like ours? Did the good guys win?"

"We did. Two of them, wars that is, but planes were used more in the second one. But that was 70 years ago. When the technology for planes was brought through the door that was during or just after the war. And from what I can tell, that airfield was mostly used for leisure flying and as a flight school. It didn't get big airplanes."

"What about who won?" pressed Trice.

"Our side won. But there were heavy losses on both sides, and a lot of civilians killed in horrible ways." She didn't know how to bring up the atrocities of the Second World War with these people from another world that she had just met.

"So the side with the aeros won!" crowed Trice.

"Both sides had planes," Cassidy explained. "In fact, it could be argued that the other side had better engines in some cases."

Breen said quietly, "They keep telling us we'll win because of the aeros."

"I can't really predict anything like that. I'm not an expert in planes or the wars of my world. I wouldn't be able to say anything on battle strategies and why one side won and one side didn't. There have been other wars, but nothing on the same scale."

The three considered this and Breen commented, "I hope we win."

That seemed to end the conversation, and all four of them started to pick up their dishes. Cassidy figured it was best if she just headed back to her room. She had caused enough trouble and didn't want to cause more problems. If she did, they might march her back to the portal and she'd never finish her mission. Bored, she laid on her bed and eventually drifted off to sleep.

CHAPTER TEN

For the next two days, Cassidy heard nothing from Shari. She was starting to worry that the flight director had forgotten about her. She would go to the mess hall at meal times, usually lingering over a hot drink or slowly picking at her food. Sometimes someone would sit with her, and they would have some idle chit chat. She wasn't feeling the same connection she had with Margaretta and Phia, or perhaps she was purposefully keeping herself distant. Trice would often make a point to sit with her and chat. At first, she thought there might be some sort of attraction, but really, it seemed that he was just grateful for her role in making flights around the island safer. They would talk, but he often wanted to talk about airplanes in greater detail than Cassidy was familiar with, and she was often lost in his questions and explanations.

At supper on the second day, Cassidy had arrived at the mess hall early, as she was wont to do with nothing else to occupy her time, and as she was trying yet another mystery food, Trice almost bounded over to her.

"Cassidy! I have amazing news!"

His smile was huge. She noticed he hadn't even picked

up his food before coming to talk to her. She looked up at him, and he pulled out the chair opposite to her.

"Flight Director Spear said I can take you on a flight around the island!"

Cassidy was shocked, "She said what? Why?"

"I was given the assignment to test the new nav equipment and fly around the island. I don't know, maybe they hope we can start to map this place or something. But I have the most flight hours of anyone currently on crew, and most of those are supply runs to and from the island, so she figured I should get to test it. And she suggested I take you. As a reward! Isn't that amazing?!"

He was thrilled with the idea. So was Cassidy. She was tired of being cooped up with nothing to do. At least when she was stuck on an archaeological site she was finding artifacts or fixing equipment or something. Laying around, literally, was torture.

"So I'll get to see the island?" she asked.

"Yeah! We'll go tomorrow just after first light. Grab some extra food to take back to your room so you can eat in the morning. It's not regulation, but it's what we all do. We should be back before lunch, but I'll get meal kits just in case." He beamed at her again. "I can't wait!"

With that, he dashed off to get in line for food. A few minutes later he was back with Breen, talking to him just as excitedly about the flight.

"So, it's not like it's top secret; they wouldn't tell me that beforehand," Trice was explaining as he sat down. "I'm to test the new nav equipment and see if there is the probability that we might be able to map this island." He turned to Cassidy. "There isn't even a map to this island.

How absolutely ridiculous is that? But we've never had the equipment to do it."

Cassidy listened and wondered why a magnetic compass was their only option. She thought about the time she was on a site and they didn't have a working compass. A bunch of archaeologists and not one working compass between them was a story in itself, but they had a geometry set for drawing maps and used the protractor to create a map. It was painfully slow, but it was an isolated dig and a two day drive to the nearest shop. The biggest problem was that they couldn't orient the map in the real world. That was easily fixed on the next supply run, but without a compass, there was no way to do it right. She could only imagine the difficulty of flying, where navigation was so important.

"Alright, Cassidy," Trice declared. "Get that extra food and head off. We'll be up early."

With that, he shoved back his chair, walked to the desserts, picked up a few things, and left. Cassidy liked his idea of breakfast, and followed his lead.

***

The next morning, Cassidy stood outside of her quarters, unsure where to go. The sky was starting to lighten and she was worried about missing the flight. Next thing, Breen was running toward her, carrying a small bag.

"I figured Trice forgot you didn't know your way around. While he's a great pilot, he sometimes gets a little too focused on the flight and forgets about silly things like that. It's a good thing someone else has to worry about his logistics..." Breen handed her the bag. "Here's a lunch, in case he forgot one for you. I doubt it, he might forget everything else, but not food. Come on."

Breen led the way across the base to the airfield. The doors to the second hangar were open, and a crew were bringing out an aircraft. Trice was watching, holding a clipboard and directing the crew.

"Trice!" Breen called. "You forgot about Cassidy!"

Trice turned and waved. "What? Really? Well, thanks for bringing her. Hey Cassidy. I picked up your lunch."

Cassidy and Breen shared a smile.

"Hi. Thanks, Breen, for showing me where to go."

"No trouble. Be safe, don't let him show off too much."

"I won't," Cassidy said as Breen turned and ran off, probably to head off to wherever he was supposed to actually be.

Cassidy turned to Trice. "So, what can I do?"

Trice glanced at his clipboard, the airplane, then at her. "I think maybe see if one of the flying suits fit you. You'll be more comfortable. Just haul it over your regular clothes."

Cassidy found a number of dull, grey coveralls hung on pegs along a back wall. She sorted through them, looking for one in her size. After trying on two, the third fit comfortably enough. She was buttoning the suit as she walked back to Trice.

"That looks like it fits well," he said. "The aeroplane is ready to go, and I have all of the outside safety checks done. Let's climb in and I'll start the next batch of checks."

"I am glad to see that there are a lot of safety checks. That makes me much more comfortable."

"Why? Do they not do safety checks where you are from?"

Cassidy laughed a little. "Oh, I am sure they do, just I only fly commercial, so it's rare that I see them do it. I only saw the full rigmarole of checks when I was in a heli…" Cassidy cut herself off. It was bad enough she had mentioned jet engines; she didn't want to have to explain helicopters! "When I was flying with military craft. On commercial flights, the passengers aren't really privy to the safety checks, except for what we should do in case of emergency."

"In case of emergency? I think if the planes goes down we just need to hold on and hope for the best."

"I think that's the same basic idea as the emergency briefings on commercial flights, but if people are told what they should do, it makes them feel less helpless, and maybe bracing for an impact will help some people survive. I really think it's more about the oxygen masks and emergency exits."

Trice considered this. "Well, we're not going high enough to need air, but there will be a canister and mask next to your seat. As for emergency exits," he indicated the plane itself, "wherever and however you can get out, I guess."

Cassidy wanted to ask about parachutes, but guessed if they had them she would have been told.

They walked over to the airplane and Trice directed Cassidy to get in first.

"You'll sit in the second seat, and I'll be in the front with the controls. You have some controls, but don't touch them." He handed her a compass. "Here's some nav for you. The flight director thinks you'll be a good second set of eyes. You know how to use this?"

Cassidy was surprised that Trice's nav equipment just looked like a simple compass. But, then again, magnetic compasses had not really changed in her own world in thousands of years, so why would they really be any different here? She pulled out her own compass to compare. Hers was wavering back and forth, as it had been since she arrived, but the one from Trice was focused on a single point.

"Oh, you have an old one? Looks a little different, and it's doing that strange thing. So, our plan is to circumnavigate the island, then fly in both of those directions," he indicated Cassidy's compass, "and see what the difference is."

Cassidy nodded, and started to work on strapping herself into her seat. Trice pulled himself into the cockpit, strapped himself in and tapped a few dials.

"I'm going to start the engines. It will be a bit loud so we won't be able to talk. Are you ready?"

"Ready as ever," Cassidy replied. She thought back to the din from the prop plane to Fredericton as she pulled a small waterproof notebook out her bag and pencil. She figured she might as well take some notes while in the air.

"Here we go!" Trice whooped and the engines roared to life. Cassidy listened as he revved one, then the other, then left both running with a steady hum. She chuckled to herself at how quiet they were, though Trice thought of them as loud. With a jerk, the plane started forward, slowly at first, then picking up speed. After a few little bumps, the aircraft started to lift off. Cassidy looked out the window and watched as they climbed. A straight run from the airfield took them out over the water. After another minute or so of climbing, Trice banked the aircraft to the left. He circled back over the base. Cassidy had not realized how close to the water it was, but it was almost on the shore. In Cassidy's opinion, the plane still felt very low, but Trice seemed to be keeping it steady. They flew along the coast and within minutes were over the village. Cassidy felt like if they were just a little closer she would be able to identify people. Funny how moments ago she felt too low, and now found that flying so close to the ground was exhilarating! She held two fingers on her pulse. It was certainly up a little. Once the initial thrill passed, she glanced down at the compasses she had in front of her. The one Trice had given her was still pointing true, and she guessed that it must be the pole for this world; whether that was north or what, she did not know as the arm for the compass that was pointing in that direction was painted black and the other half was unpainted and was a light silver. There wasn't a handy little N like on the tip of her compass to say north, but then again, with the translation, it's not like she actually knew the word they might use for north. The little circle on the end of the black tip she could be seeing as an "O" or it could just be a random symbol; she couldn't be certain. Her compass was still wavering back and forth, but she noted that one side of that arc was in the same direction as the fixed compass. So hers was obviously trying to point to the pole, but something on the island was keeping it from staying true to the pole. She wondered if it was something that would interact with the mineral from the statue and that's why it would interfere, or, if she was really lucky, perhaps it was more of the mineral. If it were, if nothing else, she would have to make sure she got a sample to bring back to Gamgee.

The flight was wonderful. Trice kept them close to the coastline, which was amazing to watch. The island was so diverse. Sometimes there would be a luxurious-looking beach, dotted with small boats and people out with fishing nets, casting them into the water. Then the coast would get a bit rocky and change to forest, with trees almost hanging out over the water, reaching for the sunshine. In the interior, the island seemed to be mostly forest, with thick trees covering most of the land, except for a few breaks in the trees that opened up to bodies of water. Trice took the plane up, and Cassidy could see that the island was not very big at all, likely hardly a day's walk to cross it, and two rivers created a large, meandering X through the island, meeting in almost the middle in a large pond. She wished she had a camera as it was beautiful. Instead, she used the compass to do a rough sketch in her notebook and made a few notes to possibly be able to do a better sketch later on. If only Jameson could see her, voluntarily drawing a map without any complaints at all! Then she thought about how she would probably have to make a copy of it for the base, and realized it would be a heck of a lot of work and she would make sure she didn't tell Jameson at all. Next dig he might expect her to keep the site plan, and that was just too much fine work and small measurements for her liking.

As promised, Trice took them for a flight around the

outside of the island. He changed altitude a couple of times, and Cassidy could not figure out exactly what the reason for the change was, but it was nice to get the different perspectives. She noted that her compass kept trying to point to one spot that seemed like it was relatively central to the island, but from the air she could not see what that might be. It all just looked like forest. She wondered where, in all of the trees, would she find the door.

Back over the base again, Trice flew in low and, for a moment, Cassidy thought they were going to land, but, no, he just waggled his wings and took off again, this time to the centre of the island. They flew straight across, not quite following one of the rivers, but as it wandered, the river did pass under them a couple of times. It looked like the river ultimately came out next to the village, which made sense from a settlement point of view as it would be a good source of fresh water. They crossed the entire island and Cassidy worked with her rough map and the two compasses to try to get an even better idea of the source of the interference. She narrowed it down to a fairly broad area just off from the central pond, away from any of the major branches of rivers.

Once they passed the island, Trice brought the plane higher, and they crossed the water and they flew over the mainland a little. Cassidy was again shocked at how little water separated the island from the mainland, for such an independent attitude. She thought it would be like Hawaii relative to the continental United States, but in fact, she guessed, on a clear day, one would be able to see the mainland from the coast. Now, the village was on the opposite side from the mainland, as far away as possible, which likely led to some of that feeling of isolation.

Along the coast, they passed over a small town. It was about twice the size of the island village, but still not very big at all. Trice again went in low and waggled his wings over the town. She guessed there was a good chance that he was from the area. Cassidy also wondered for a moment if it was the same village that Shari was from, remembering that she said she was from a small town herself. But then again, depending on how large the country was, there could be countless small towns and villages all along the coast, let alone the ones that would be further inland.

Once past the village, Trice turned back, circling over the continent until they lined up almost exactly with one of the major rivers on the island. He kept his altitude low, crossed the water, and came back over the island.

Suddenly, there was a loud pop and the entire plane shook. Cassidy looked out the side of the aircraft just in time to hear the rip of metal and see a large piece of the engine cowling fly away. A bright light seemed to almost slither out of the engine and the propeller slowed and then stopped turning. She looked to the other side, and the propeller was still turning, but stuttering, and she assumed it must be struggling as the only one working. The damaged engine was glowing brightly and licks of fire were coming out of the engine. They were falling, and fast.

CHAPTER ELEVEN

Cassidy's pulse roared in her ears. She could feel the rush of adrenaline and tingled all over. She savoured it for a millisecond before she checked her straps and wondered about all of the safety demonstrations she had seen in airplanes. She had even read the information cards from time to time, when a flight was particularly boring and she had run out of absolutely everything else to do. Should she brace herself? Her seat was further back from Trice's than in a commercial plane. Would it help? At the same time, she found she kept wanting to watch what was happening outside. The other engine seemed to be fighting to keep turning, but just could not keep the plane in the air. That light was just starting around the propeller, and she could see as the smooth circle of the propeller would occasionally stutter. Not that it mattered, the one propeller could not keep them in the air. Trice was fighting with the plane, trying, with some success, to keep it from spiralling toward the ground. As the other propeller stopped, they stopped spinning toward the earth, and Trice managed to tilt the aircraft a little forward, so it wasn't barrelling nose-first at the ground. The trees came up to meet them just as Trice straightened up the plane, and Cassidy heard the tops of the trees break against the metal as she felt the aircraft shudder. She saw part of a tree lodged in the broken engine, the flame licking at its branches. The plane continued to push forward, and now the trees were at eye level, reaching for the metal intruder. It seemed they were grabbing at the plane, each branch slowing the bird as it wanted to land. Cassidy was thrown in her seat as a wing collided with a large tree. The wing ripped off with such ease that it reminded Cassidy of ripping a piece of aluminum foil. The plane continued on, leaving the wing behind. As another tree grabbed the other wing, the airplane turned, circling around the tree until they were turned completely around before they escaped the tree and the airplane continued to fly, but backward. Cassidy bent over, thinking about the brace position, now not knowing what might be coming, and put her arms out to just barely touch Trice's chair ahead of her. She did it just in time, as the plane came to a sudden and violent stop and she was thrown forward. She was thankful that she had just put her hands forward, as they protected her head somewhat as she was pushed forward. The harness did grab her, and she knew she would be bruised.

Finally, the airplane stopped. Cassidy stayed still for a few breaths and felt her blood rush before she sat up and called Trice.

"Are you okay?" she asked.

Trice moaned and Cassidy knew he was alive but was afraid for how hurt he might be.

"I'm fine. I struck the dashboard, I think I'm bleeding, and I am going to have a lot of bruises."

"Yeah, me too," Cassidy replied.

"Cassidy, I am so sorry."

"I'm bruised, but otherwise okay. Nothing to be sorry about. Unless you crashed the plane on purpose, and that engine makes me think you didn't," Cassidy replied, trying for joking, but coming off a little tersely.

Trice was a little cowed, then defensive. "I would never try to crash a plane. I don't know what happened. Something must have gotten into the engine, or it was faulty. I've flown this one before, and all the checks were fine."

Cassidy took a deep breath. "Yes, I know it's not your fault. I meant that as a joke. I guess it's hard to joke after a plane crash."

They both looked at each other, then untangled themselves from their straps and clamored out of the plane. They each took a few steps out of the aircraft before turning around and examining the wreckage.

"So I guess we walk?" Cassidy asked.

Without answering, Trice went back to the plane. The engines were still bright, but they didn't seem to be flaming anymore. Cassidy walked back toward the aircraft while Trice rummaged around in the aircraft for a moment. She bent down and picked up a small sliver of glowing stone, its light fading quickly. She pocketed it just before Trice emerged from the wreckage with Cassidy's bag, and three bags of lunch.

"First, we eat!" he declared. "And thanks to Breen, we have an extra lunch to share!"

"Maybe we should save that one in case the walk out is more difficult?" Cassidy asked.

Trice started spreading out the contents of the bags.

"Let's eat the buns first, they're filled with cream that could go bad."

Cassidy doubted they were actually called buns, or, given that nothing she'd had in this place tasted like dairy, cream, but the offered food looked like a steamed bun, so she guessed her translator decided that was the best fit. At least it had an easier time with the military folks who seemed to use fewer colloquialisms; even those from the island. Whatever it was, Cassidy took the offered food and enjoyed the softness of it, and the creamy meat and vegetable filled inside. She thought it was almost like a chicken pot pie in a potato crust. Almost.

They went through the rest of the food. There were some soft pieces of fruit that they also ate, and some harder fruit that they put back in a sack and put in Cassidy's bag. There were canteens of juice, and they took one each and Trice attached the third to his belt. The sun was hot, so they agreed that it would be wise to follow the river and refill the canteens as needed. Trice assured her that the river water was fine to drink, and likely she had been drinking it the entire time as there was no sort of water treatment on the island.

"We don't have any in my town either, but when you get to the bigger towns and cities, they can't drink river water, it's too dirty," he explained.

"I think in some areas it can still be like that where I'm from, but there is a lot of pollution and so a lot of smaller, more isolated places have a lot of trouble getting clean water."

"We have some places like that too. It is sad."

Finally, they each took a sort of cookie, and wrapped

the others in a different sack to put in Cassidy's bag. Sweet treats in hand, they consulted the compasses.

"Mine doesn't seem to be wavering as much from here, so whatever is causing the interference must be in the same direction as the magnetic pole," Cassidy deduced.

"If that's the case, we can do better on our mission and maybe find out what's causing the problem. Especially if it's on the way. They're not expecting us for a bit, but they might have heard the crash. It's not a big island, but we are pretty far off from the base. Search missions aren't easy here, with whatever the problem is, and if they think it made the plane crash, they might hesitate about a fly over. But, just in case..."

Trice jumped to his feet and ran back to the downed plane. He rummaged in the wreckage, around Cassidy's seat, and came back with a small pot.

"Standard on all planes is a pot of paint so we can say which way we're going!" He called to Cassidy.

Cassidy wandered over as Trice unscrewed the top and climbed up on the wreckage.

"If I paint our direction here, it will let them know where we're going. Which way are we going?"

Cassidy pointed along the angle her compass would sometimes point to, thinking they'd go that way then follow the pole. Trice, on the aircraft, was talking partly to himself and partly to Cassidy.

"So this means we're going that way. And this means we're uninjured, relatively speaking of course, and this means two people... There!" He hopped down. "Ready to go!"

Trice's excitement was catching. They had just survived a plane crash and now were going to discover the great mystery of the island. While she was a bit sore, and expected to be very sore tomorrow, for right now there were things to do. This was the most excitement she'd had in days. Weeks even, as finding artifacts was nowhere as exhilarating as surviving a plane crash! They picked up their supplies, and, with Cassidy and her compass leading the way, they set off into the trees.

The crash had obviously done a fair bit of damage, creating a bit of a clearing with the impact, and breaking trees as it came in to land. Most of that was in the opposite direction, but newly broken pieces of trees could be seen clinging in the forest ahead of them. Flying debris had further damaged some of the trees. It looked like part of the tail must have whipped forward when the aircraft turned when it went around that one large tree, and Cassidy saw the piece had ripped through the branches of two trees, cutting the branches away, before embedding itself into the trunk of a third. She took a moment to just stare at it, and really contemplate how lucky they were to be alive. Her heart beat a little faster and her fingertips tingled just thinking of the crash again.

Once out of the debris field, the trees were close together, but far enough apart that they could easily walk through the forest. There was a slight bit of leaf litter, surprising for the number of leafy trees, but Cassidy supposed it was the equivalent to summer. In the fall, it would be much more difficult to navigate the trees if all these leaves were to fall. They both watched their footing, and even so would still stumble over the odd branch.

After about an hour of easy walking, the foliage

changed, and they found themselves faced with a tangle of bushes about the height of themselves. It was thick and difficult to pass through, and they each tried to fight their way through the branches. Any gentle conversation they were having stopped as now communication consisted of grunts of effort, and the occasional "Watch your eyes!" when someone would let go of a branch and it would fly back toward the other person. Cassidy wished for a machete or some other tool to be able to cut through the thick, wooden plants that tugged at her boots and tangled in her hair.

"Stop!" Cassidy called suddenly.

"What? Are you okay?" Trice asked with concern.

"I dropped the compass! I was trying to check it"

"It's okay, we'll find it. Somehow," Trice sighed.

They both crouched down as best they could in the brambles and started to search through the plants. The branches tore at their hands, and they tore back, ripping at the branches. Cassidy produced a pocket knife and started cutting at some of the smaller branches, trying to throw them away, but often just managing to get the branches tangled in others nearby.

"Got it!" Cassidy cried, pulling her hand up from the tangle. She opened her hand, to find a round rock. With a sigh, they kept searching.

"I think I actually have it this time," Trice chided as he stretched his fingers into a small opening near the base of one plant, and pulled out the compass!

Cassidy thanked him, and took it back. She carefully checked it, then put it in her pocket. "I think I'll keep this in my pocket until we get out of this mess. But it looks like we've been going in a pretty straight line, so let's keep going this way." She pointed, and went back to fighting through the bushes.

Suddenly, Cassidy burst out of the tangled shrubs. They stopped suddenly just a few steps from the bank of a river. With a struggle, Trice pushed his way out, stumbled, and caught himself before he fell into the river.

"Those bushes are crazy! I have never had to push my way through something like those before! I hope no one else at the base ever finds them, because they might bring them into training!"

"I've had to deal with something similar before, when I was working in a boreal forest, but those were even worse and more tangled than anything I have ever dealt with." Cassidy took a moment to catch her breath, then decided to just sit and take a proper rest.

"Good idea," declared Trice as he unhooked his canteen and drank deep. Cassidy did the same, and within a few minutes, both had drained their containers and crawled to the stream to refill them. The water was refreshing and cool against Cassidy's hand, so once her canteen was filled, she reached both hands into the clear water, pooled them, and splashed some on her face. She reached down, pooled her hands again, and lifted the water, drinking some. It was refreshing inside and out.

She wasn't sure if she had ever seen water so clear in a deep stream. Certainly she had seen clear streams before, where you could see the bottom and see fish swimming past, but this seemed even clearer, like the water was almost magnifying what she could see. It was magical to watch a snail slowly crawl along a rock. After a few minutes she felt rested, and turned to Trice.

"Ready to go again?"

"After you hand me a plum."

"A what?" she thought she heard right, but nothing in the bag looked like plum. Another mistranslation.

"The fruit you have in your bag," he explained.

"Oh," Cassidy responded as she brought her bag in front of her and searched for the fruit. "I haven't figured out the names for many of the fruits or vegetables here. Everyone just assumes I know what everything is."

Trice took the piece of fruit and bit into it. "That's understandable," he said in between bites. "You're speaking the same language, so it's easy to forget that you're not from here. You just have a different dialect, so it sounds like you're from another part of the country, not a whole other world."

"Hmmm... yeah, fair. I sometimes forget I'm speaking a different language, because I only hear my native tongue."

"Weird," Trice said as he gave her a considering look.

Cassidy looked away and picked up her own plum and started to eat. When he was done, Trice threw the stone from his fruit back into the tangle of branches. Cassidy decided to put hers back in the sack and back in her bag. While she didn't like the mess of branches, she also didn't want to be the one to introduce a potentially invasive species to the island. She had seen enough climatological devastation; she didn't want to be the cause of it. It was probably a wasted effort though, as who knows what the base was doing with their food. Plus, for all she knew, plums, or whatever they were, grew on the island.

"Ready to go?" Trice asked.

"Sure." Cassidy pulled out the two compasses. Her was wavering more than back at the plane crash, so they had obviously veered from the pole, and thus from the base because the base seemed to be in that direction. From her aerial view, they could just follow the river and come out around the village. Her compass said they had to cross the river to find whatever it was.

"Ready to get wet?" Cassidy asked.

Trice looked down at his boots. "Guess so," he said.

They both bent down and took off their boots and rolled up their pants. Boots in hand, Cassidy sucked in air as her feet touched the cold water. The river wasn't very wide, maybe fifteen meters at most, but each step had to be taken carefully on the slippery rocks. As she walked across, the water kept rising until it was licking at her pants, rolled up to her knees. She started to bend down to further roll up her pants, but as she bent, her bag shifted and she worried about losing it or her balance, so she straightened up and kept going, even if it meant wet pants.

They both splashed along and made it across the river without incident. Cassidy rolled her pants back down and laughed quietly to herself, looking at the stripes of water across her legs. At least it was a warm day, and her pants should dry quickly. She put on her socks and boots and finished tying her laces as Trice finished his. She checked the compass again, pointed the direction, and they both set off again.

This side of the river was even easier to navigate than before, without a tangle of bushes. The area was very open, with only a few trees with large canopies shading them as they walked. Colourful flowers with long, teardrop petals hugged the trees. Cassidy thought the area looked like a park it was so beautiful. Looking up through the canopy, the sun was high, around its apex, telling them half the day had passed, but they still had hours of light left. She was thankful for the light covering of leaves, especially because she didn't have a hat with her to help protect her fair skin.

The two almost strolled through the grove, not wanting to rush, but at the same time taking advantage of the easy walking conditions. About a half hour in, they came across a small stream, flowing toward the river. Cassidy checked the compass again, and noticed they had gone off course. The leisurely walk was a little too much so, she guessed. The compass pointed along the tributary, and so they walked upstream. The stream started to widen, but was still narrow enough that Cassidy guessed she could jump across it if she wanted. Still, it was an easy walk. After some time, more flowers started to appear along the shore, leafy green plants with soft pink flowers clung to the bank of the stream.

Cassidy noticed a noise and looked up from the flowers, and saw that the little stream flowed from a small pond surrounded by flowers and flowing trees, and soft white blossoms dropped from the trees to float in the pond. At the head of the pond was a cascading waterfall that was still far enough away to barely be heard. It was a beautiful sight, a little piece of paradise.

CHAPTER TWELVE

Cassidy had seen some beautiful places in her life, on her world and others, but this small oasis was perhaps one of the most amazing. The small pond was crystal clear. She could see the red, blue, green, purple, and black rocks right on the bottom. Bright green plants stood between some of the rocks, waving gently as orange, red, and yellow fish darted among them. The pond itself wasn't very big, maybe ten meters across, if that, and almost perfectly round. The coloured rocks extended on to the shore, expanding outward until they were blanketed by a bright green, thick, moss-like plant with small pink flowers. The moss gave way to a variety of brightly coloured flowers of every colour and shape, which in turn, gave way to lush, flowering trees. The large white blossoms weighed heavily on the branches, and fallen flowers floated on the pond's surface. At the head of the pond was a waterfall, which created a small basin of churning water.

The crash of the waterfall was not loud by the river, in fact, she could still hear the burble of the stream along with the waterfall. The sheet of water was falling from a high peak, a small mountain that created a shear wall just behind the pond. The cliff seemed to extend back into the forest, and out of view. Cassidy sat at the edge of the pond. The moss was soft and the rocks smooth. She took out her notebook and started sketching the area. Trice came and sat next to her, watching her draw, occasionally pointing out a detail she missed. The drawing wasn't to scale, but she had to record the spot. Then they worked together to draw a rough map of where they crashed, the larger river, and this small pond. Cassidy used the changes in the compass headings to estimate the meanderings of the bodies of water, and the corrected compass to estimate the direction of the village and the base.

"Looks like your nav is pointing right at the waterfall. It's hardly even moving toward the pole now," Trice observed.

"Hopefully whatever is causing the pull is near or even behind the waterfall. If it's up the hill, I don't think we'll be able to find it. Do you think we'd be able to come back with climbing gear?" Cassidy liked the idea of climbing that rock face and seeing the island from up high. That would be a thrill. Not that from the airplane wasn't up high, but from the top of the hill she would be able to potentially see more landmarks that she would have missed from the plane.

"Don't see why not. Well, if we get permission that is."

"Oh, yeah. Permission," mused Cassidy as she wondered if she could come back without the base's blessing. "Anyway, it might be a moot question anyway. Let's see what's at the waterfall."

Cassidy closed her notebook and tossed it in her bag.

She stood up, brushed the moss from her pants and started around the pond. Trice followed a step behind.

The rock wall made only a small ledge between itself and the pond, and the two had to pick across carefully. The pond looked fairly deep at this end, but with the water so clear, it was difficult to guess how deep it might be. Twice Cassidy's foot slid off the ledge and she got a little wet. The water was frigid, and the cold shocked her each time, but she kept her balance and managed to find secure enough hand holds to not fall in. Trice had a little more trouble and came close to falling, splashing up to one of his knees before he managed to find somewhere to grab on and pull himself back up. He cursed the cold of the water. Not that it would have been a huge concern had they gotten wet, but it was cold enough that it would take some time to warm up after.

The entire effort to stay dry was wasted when the waterfall was so close to the rock that they both had to go through it to see if there was something behind it. Cassidy got through to find a small opening, just big enough to walk through if she turned sideways. She went through, and Trice followed moments later.

"Given how wet we ended up getting, we should have just swum across the pond!" Cassidy exclaimed as she twisted her hair, trying to get some of the water out.

"Guess we'll just save ourselves the trouble and swim out," Trice decided. "Now, where are we?"

They looked around the small cave. They had no light source, but the waterfall was thin enough that the light could get in. They waited a moment for their eyes to adjust. It took Cassidy a moment to realize that her eyes weren't failing to adjust, but the cave was full of black rocks. She walked forward and touched one of the rocks. It was smooth, almost glassy. She tried to pick up a rock, but it resisted. She pulled harder, until it came away and she could hold it in her hand. It was like pulling two magnets apart! She brought the rock back down to where it had been, and could feel the pull. She opened her hand, flattening her palm, and tilted it just a little, not enough that gravity should take the rock, but it still rolled off her hand and stuck fast to the other rocks again. Cassidy picked up the piece again, and walked back toward the light of the waterfall. It was black, just like the rock inside of the statue!

Meanwhile, Trice had wandered further into the cave. Cassidy could not see where he went, but also wasn't really paying attention. She was wondering just how much of the rock was there. She guessed this was the source of the interference. She pulled out her compass and stood in the middle of the rocks. The light was poor, but she could just see the white of the compass point. It was still. She turned. And it still didn't move. She moved around in a circle. Nothing. She must be right in the centre of all of the magnetic rock. For it to have caused such a problem on the island, it must be a huge source of it! Perhaps more than enough for the flight director to fix all of the aircraft, and give the statue back to the village! Cassidy remembered her mission and took a few chunks of rock and put them in her pockets for herself. She put two smaller pieces in one pocket, and, when she reached back in that pocket, found they had fused together.

"What amazing properties to this rock," she muttered

to herself. "There are pebbles and small stones around that haven't fused, but the two pieces I just put in my pocket fused."

She picked up another two pieces, and when she brought them together, they too fused. She thought how she wished her geology were better, but then she doubted anything like this existed on her world.

"Cassidy, come check this out," Trice called from deep in the cavern.

Cassidy carefully picked her way through the cave. As she went further, she really wanted some sort of lantern, but theirs had been destroyed in the crash and the batteries for her small flashlight were dead. The cave grew darker, the black stones seeming to consume the light. When she moved too close to a pile of rocks, she could feel the stones in her pocket pull toward them. She considered removing them and getting some later, but given how things went so unpredictably with the village and the base before, she thought it best to get her sample for Dr. Gamgee now. The cave had become so dark that she could not see in front of her. Just to check, she waved a hand in front of her face, and, knowing it was there, could not see it. She wasn't sure what Trice could be showing her in the pitch black, but she shuffled on, trying to stick to the path that seemed to flow through the rocks.

Moments later, she noticed that she could see again. Just the barest outline of the rocks ahead of her, but she could see. She brought her hand up, and sure enough, she could see it. She kept moving forward, and as the light increased, so did the confidence in her steps. The rocks were changing too. Some of them had what looked like snowflakes on them. She looked closer, and they were small occlusions of a white rock. As she kept going, the white became more prominent until the rocks were covered in it, just like the quartz-like material on the outside of the statue from the village! She found Trice at a wide entrance, standing in the sunshine.

"Don't get too close," he said and pointed downward.

Cassidy looked, and it seemed that the hill they were in did not end gradually, but rather was a sheer cliff. She wondered if the ground had dropped away, or if they had gradually climbed while inside the cave. Either way, they were well above the tree tops. Cassidy stepped back from the ledge, and took out her compass again. Hers was pointing directly behind her, at the stones. No surprise there, she thought. The other compass, the one from the base, seemed to not quite be corrected enough, because it seemed to be struggling to point away from the rocks.

"I wonder how far we've gone; it didn't seem that far through the mountain," Cassidy mused.

"I doubt it is very far because I've never noticed this from the air, and you'd think a big line of rock like this would be noticeable. I am still curious about the source of that waterfall, even more now that I know the hill is so narrow."

"Yeah, it would almost have to be a very deep pond to create it, or, I don't know." In all honesty, Cassidy had forgotten about the waterfall, she was so absorbed in finding a source of these rocks.

"The story!" she exclaimed.

"What?" Trice looked at her, confused.

"The story about the idol. The statue. Margaretta told it to me about their ancestor who found the statue. He must have stopped somewhere under here to rest when he was hunting. I bet there is a giant rock down there that looks like a sleeping beast. Down there must be the spot where he found the stone, and no one has found any since because they're behind the waterfall and up this cliff. The one he found must have fallen down from in here."

"So this is the same stuff as the statue? The same stuff used to fix the nav equipment?" Trice asked.

"It is! This solves everything! There's so much of it that all the planes can be fixed, and the village can get their statue back!" Cassidy was thrilled.

Trice picked up one of the white stones. "Do you have much room in your bag? Maybe we should bring some of this back?"

Cassidy agreed and picked a couple of fist-sized rocks that could easily fit in her bag. She had a bandana with her and wrapped a few in it to make it easier to carry. Trice picked up his own rock.

"I'll take some from the other side of the cavern as well. Well, I guess I'll take one, because if I put in a few, they'll just turn into one if they come into contact with each other."

Trice looked confused again and Cassidy explained the strange magnetism of the rocks, and how that seemed to be the thing that fixed the compass to negate the interference caused by the mineral. Trice seemed to understand, or at least understood as much as Cassidy did, as she still couldn't quite explain the physics behind the phenomenon. She'd leave that for Dr. Gamgee to understand.

Cassidy regretted leaving her bag back by the pond. It would have been nice to have been able to sketch the view from the opening, but she would just have to try to remember it to do a basic drawing. What she really wanted was a camera because no drawing she could do would do it justice. They both sat at the edge of the cliff for a little while, just enjoying the view.

It was Trice who decided they should start making their way back.

"We know where this is now, we can show people the way, but we should get moving if we want to make it back before dark."

Cassidy agreed, and they made their way back through the tunnel. Cassidy picked up another of the black stones and put it in her clutch, and Trice played with some of the smaller ones, examining how they pull towards each other before putting a piece in his own pocket. Even though they had both thought it easier to swim, they opted for the more difficult route out of the cave, and again picked their way across the lip of the pond. Once safely on solid ground again, and only a little wet this time, Cassidy looked back at the pond. Now that she was looking for it, she could see, in amongst the red and purple rocks, the black magnetic rocks. They were so distinct, she wondered how she missed them in the first place.

Back at her bag, they had a quick snack and Cassidy went to transfer her bandana full of stones to her bag. The ones covered in the quartz-like material didn't fuse, the outer shell likely blocking some of the magnetism. She took out one covered stone, and one uncovered one, and placed them in front of her, at about 10 and 2 on a clock. She took out her compass and brought it closer to them.

While the needle was certainly still being pulled by the massive amount of material behind the waterfall, it did seem to be a little more attracted to the uncovered mineral instead of the covered one. She found this interesting, and put both of the rocks back in her bag and pocketed her compass.

Everything packed up, they decided to follow the stream. It would lead back to the river, which in turn, would lead to the village. Certainly they could use the fixed compass to walk in a straight line, but walking along the river bank seemed like it would be much easier than trying to sort through anything like that mess of woody shrubs that they had encountered on their way from the crash.

The walk out was uneventful, almost peaceful, if not a little rushed. Trice, even knowing there was still food left in Cassidy's bag, was pushing to get back to the base before the mess closed that evening. Cassidy reminded him that he would likely be called in to be debriefed and might still miss supper, which only made him hike faster. He set a rigorous pace and all conversation ceased as Cassidy tried to keep up. She was fit, but wasn't doing regular military drills like he was. At one point, while walking back along the main river, Cassidy recognized an area and thought the door might be close by. For a moment, she debated just leaving with her samples and putting this world and its complications behind her, but decided against it. It would be wrong to leave the village, especially after the kindness they showed her. Leaving would be easy, but not right.

That also meant they were close to the village, and back to safety. Maybe even in time to eat.

CHAPTER THIRTEEN

As predicted, they came out of the woods on the other side of the village from the base.

It was Rim who saw them first, and the child rushed over.

"Cassidy! You're back!" Rim exclaimed.

"No, not really. We were just lost in the woods. But I found the most amazing thing!" Cassidy started to explain until Trice cut in.

"Cassidy, we were on a military mission and what we found is a military matter." He was all authority, very different from the Trice she had been talking to over the past few days. "I must forbid you to talk about our mission and what was found."

"But this will fix everything."

"That is not for you to decide. If you do not come to the base now, I will tell the flight director and you will be removed to the base."

Cassidy saw how serious he was, and how he was scaring Rim. She leaned down and gave Rim a comforting hug and whispered, "Give this to Margaretta," and slipped a small quartz-covered stone from her pocket to the child's hand. More loudly she said, "I'm sorry Rim. We didn't mean to scare you. I have to go," and got up.

She turned to Trice, "I'm sorry, I'm not used to military protocol."

He nodded in agreement and they turned and walked across the village, Cassidy careful to not make eye contact with anyone lest they try to talk and Trice scare them again. Once they were away from the village, Trice turned to her.

"I'm sorry for that, too. I know you're not military, but we do have to follow orders."

"I understand," she lied.

Once at the base, Cassidy and Trice were sent directly to Flight Director Spear's office.

"Good, you made it back. Now, report." Flight Director Spear looked at Trice.

"We departed just after first light, all checks were accomplished and everything was normal. Takeoff was normal."

As Trice spoke, Cassidy heard a clicking noise, and looked to see a stenographer behind her, taking down Trice's words. The young man would have been hidden by the door as they came in. The man was typing on a strange contraption. It was certainly similar to a typewriter, but larger. Almost like an old style typewriter for Cantonese or Japanese, complete with paper scroll at the top. Cassidy wondered if the writing style might be logographic instead of alphabetic, and she wished she could turn off the translator because watching the stenographer type seemed out of sync with what Trice was saying. Instead, she turned back to look at Trice and Shari.

"As we turned back toward the island, things were normal for a minute or two, but then the right engine shuddered. Moments later, it caught fire, the halfstone going into overglow, before the cowling ripped away. The other engine, overtaxed, gave out. We crashed, catching on trees, but landing with minimal injuries. Once assessed, we determined that the source of the interference was likely nearby, and followed the flawed navigational equipment to find the source. It was located, and we followed the main river back to the Vering Island village, passing through the village to return to the base."

"Good," responded Shari, "and the source of the interference?"

Trice produced the stones from his pocket.

"A large collection of these stones in a cave. Some are covered in a white material."

Shari examined the rocks.

"These are just like the stuff in the statue," she mused.

"Yes," Cassidy interjected. "There's a lot of it too, so you can get that and give the statue back to the village."

"Hmmm... we would have to verify it, of course, but yes, if we have another source of it, I don't see why we can't give the statue back."

Cassidy let out a sign of relief. "That's good, I thought you might have destroyed it."

"Oh, no no. We haven't destroyed it. We haven't even used any of it yet. What we have we were given by villagers who now serve. We were still only testing the material yet."

"Then why did you take it?" Cassidy exclaimed.

"Because I assumed that you telling them would not actually work. The village here is so overprotective of their superstitions and stories that they probably wouldn't have let me have it anyway."

Cassidy levelled her gaze on Flight Director Spear. "You are wrong about that," she said coldly, "they talked about it and were going to give you the statue. Instead you took it. You destroyed any goodwill that might have been left. You have made it much more difficult for you to coexist in this place because you couldn't have any faith that they would do the right thing. The villagers are good, intelligent people, and you treat them like they are clueless about the world. If you ever want to have good relations with the village again, you had better do something to make it up to them."

"I'll give back the statue. It will be fine," said Shari, a little dismissively.

"No, it won't," Cassidy responded, still very serious. "These are a people of storytellers, and if I have learned anything in my travels and studies it is that storytellers don't forget and storytellers can hold a grudge because they don't forget. You will need to make things better with them."

Shari considered this. "And how do you propose I do that?"

Cassidy paused for a moment then replied, "By bringing them in on the discovery of the cavern. No, hear me out. There is a huge source of these stones, both the covered and uncovered ones. I already know you need very little to fix the navigation equipment, and with the amount there it would take generations to use it all. Look at the statue. Yes, they put the stone back in when people die, but they lose the pieces of people who leave or die at sea, and the statue is still almost full. You need less than what they give to their own people. And this cavern is full. Trice took small samples, not the large boulders that are there. But it's also in a beautiful place. It's in a pristine environment that could be used by the people. As long as you don't destroy the place, the villagers might even help you quarry some of the stone."

"Why do you think they would help?"

"Because I have spent time with them, and they are good people who, while not looking to partake in the war, and not even completely understanding it, don't want to see people hurt," Cassidy was pleading a little now.

Shari considered Cassidy's words. "So, what you are suggesting is that I bring them to this place, and they get the place, and you think they will freely give the material we need."

"Yes," Cassidy was suddenly feeling hopeful, "approach the storytellers, the elders of the community. Take one or two of them with you, Margaretta for instance, and she will bring them around. You will all be able to work together."

"That's not really how we do things."

"Are you sure? Aren't you, as part of the defence of this place and this country, supposed to also instill a sense of patriotism in the outlying places?" Cassidy was pulling out everything she could think of from dealing with other militaries and a thesis defence she had once attended that discussed just this. "Showing cooperation will make these outlying places remember that they are part of the country, and, without that goodwill, it is much harder to recruit. If you do this right, the village will tell stories of how you impacted one of their oldest stories by finding the lost location and giving it back to the people, and they will be less afraid of the capital and more willing to volunteer. If you help them with this, you will be a hero in their stories for generations to come. Otherwise you will just be coming in with might and taking from their stories. They just want respect as the residents of this place."

Cassidy was proud of her speech and wasn't entirely certain where it came from. While she wanted to smile, she kept her face serious, but celebrated a little internally and waited for Shari's response.

Shari again considered before answering, "I... I wouldn't have thought of it that way. The biggest problem with this place is how resistant they've been."

"And it's not like you plan on leaving after the war, what with the door here," Cassidy cut in.

Shari eyed her suspiciously. "How would you know a thing like that?"

"You're not the first military I've dealt with, and the history of my own world says it has happened time and time again. So earning favour can only help you."

"You really didn't come off as this knowledgeable when we first met."

Cassidy took it in stride, "I'm aware. I don't try to cultivate it, but it usually takes me a while to figure a place out."

"Interesting... But you are right, now that the base is established, it will be permanent, and having a good working relationship with the locals will be an asset for the future." Shari paused. "And we will follow your suggestions. I will reach out to the community elders and make it a joint mission."

"May I approach Margaretta for this? She might not be receptive to you returning, and I had convinced her to let you take the statue in the first place."

Cassidy knew she was pushing it a little with that jab, but wanted to be the one to make it up to the town and to Rim, Phia, and Margaretta.

"Fine. Saves me the trouble. Get something to eat, get some sleep. Meet here at daybreak and we will make the plan, then you can go back to the village. If we're efficient, we can leave before midday. Leave the map sketches and I'll have them copied."

Cassidy handed Shari the pages from her notebook. The maps would be useful to them, but not her written notes seeing as they wouldn't be able to read them.

"Is there anything else in there I need?" Shari asked, eyeing the book.

"No, mostly notes to myself, and the last archaeological site I worked on. That last bit honestly has nothing to do with here and I need to give the notes back to my friend."

"Fine," she turned to Trice who had been so quiet Cassidy had almost forgotten about him. "Say nothing. Report here at daybreak. Dismissed."

Trice said nothing, but turned and walked out of the room.

"You too. Dismissed."

Cassidy pocketed her notebook and walked out of the room. Trice was by the door, waiting.

"Ready to eat?"

Cassidy laughed a little, even though she was disappointed that Trice had nothing to say about her speech.

"Sure, I'd love to eat."

She walked with him to the mess hall, where they just got in before the kitchen closed.

CHAPTER FOURTEEN

Cassidy felt good on her way to Shari's office. The meeting was pretty quick, mostly just to discuss the map and how long it would potentially take to get to the pond. Shari asked pointed questions about the location, how much material was present, and how difficult it would be to remove it. Cassidy and Trice answered as best they could before being dismissed. Shari and Trice would meet Cassidy and representatives from the village at the river so they could go together. Shari and Trice would collect more of the rocks, but would also start negotiations. If Cassidy was right, they could negotiate the use of the place for the villagers and the removal of the minerals for the aircraft.

Not surprisingly, Rim greeted Cassidy at the edge of the village.

"Cassidy! I gave what you gave me to Margaretta. What is it? Did it come out of the statue?"

Oh no! Cassidy thought, *I didn't think they'd assume it came out of the statue!*

"Or did it come from somewhere else? Where did it come from?" Rim prattled on.

Cassidy was a little relieved that these might just be the questions of a child.

"Rim," she asked, "could you bring me to Margaretta please?"

"Yeah, sure, of course!"

Rim led the way to Margaretta's house, telling Cassidy all about the past couple of days, especially focusing on the dessert they had for supper the night before. Cassidy had to laugh; after all of her worry over the situation, here was Rim, just worried about food. Much like Trice.

At Margaretta's house, Rim walked in and shouted, "Cassidy's here!" and ran off again.

Moments later, Margaretta and Phia appeared, and welcomed her in. The rock she had given Rim was on the living room table.

"Cassidy! Where did you find that stone? All Rim would say was that it was from you!" Margaretta asked.

"That's all I had time to say," Cassidy replied. "I was with one of the guys from the base, and he wouldn't let me say more. I had to sneak it to Rim and hoped you'd know I found a solution."

"A solution?" asked Margaretta. "Oh, to the base taking the statue. Yes, it was a shock, but in the end, it's just a statue. I understand why you left, Phia explained it, but you are welcome back here. You might get some foul looks from Carlson or Sasamuel, but that's expected. They're like that to just about everyone. So, what's this solution?"

Cassidy told them about the plane wreck and finding the beautiful pond with the waterfall and the cave behind the waterfall and how it led to a cliff. She explained how she thought that maybe they were missing a key part of the story and that this place was where Ishaul found the stone, but no one else had found one because they had never gone through the waterfall.

"We do know of that place; it's a common spot for couples to go and court, although the water is always very cold and I never heard of anyone trying to go in. There are better swimming areas."

"Well, the base wants to go and access the rocks, but they want to do it with a storyteller or two present so you can work together and maintain the area."

Margaretta paused before responding. "So, they know of this place, and instead of just taking what they want, they want to work with us? That's... that's very different from before. Cassidy? Did you say something to them?"

"I just explained how it would be good for them to work with you instead of against you. That way there might be a little more trust, and it would be easier for the villagers who work on base to face their families."

Phia cut it, "That is a good thing. We have, as a whole, not been very good to those who choose to work on the base. Not everyone wants to fish or tell stories. And we've never been that way to anyone who has left and come back."

"True as the tide," Margaretta said solemnly. "We should work together. If we work together on this, then maybe we can work together on other things."

Margaretta got up and walked to the door.

"Rim!" she called, and within moments the child appeared.

That kid has a talent, or is just really nosy, Cassidy thought.

"Please go and get the storytellers. Tell them to come here as quickly as possible," Margaretta ordered.

A few minutes later, the storytellers started coming in. True to his character, Carlson gave Cassidy a sour look. Once everyone was in, Margaretta got started.

"I had Rim send you all here because Cassidy has brought some amazing news," she started.

There was some muttering, until Margaretta produced the stone that Cassidy had given Rim the day before.

"Cassidy brought us this."

Suddenly, they were all quiet and listening. Margaretta continued.

"Yesterday, Cassidy was with someone from the base in that aeroplane that flew overhead. We didn't see it come back because it crashed."

Gertrand and Olisker shot Cassidy concerned looks.

"For those of you worried," Margaretta glared at Carlson, "Cassidy is okay, as is the one who was flying the aeroplane. One their way back, they found a cave filled with the same stones that the idol is made of. Cassidy brought one back, against the wishes of the base."

Cassidy was about to interject, but then realized that Margaretta was right, even if she didn't quite think of it that way.

"The cave is behind the waterfall at the pool, and it extends through the cliff. There's a huge chance that this is where Ishaul first found the stone we use. Speaking of which, the base is going to give back the idol. They haven't touched it yet, and want to work with us when collecting more stones."

There was some grumbling to this, from Carlson in

particular, but Gertrand shushed him and nodded for Margaretta to continue.

"They want to collect some of the stone. Cassidy says there is a lot of it behind the waterfall. But they want a couple of us to go with them to the area to make sure they also protect it so we can keep using it."

Carlson cut in. "It's our place, they have no right—"

Margaretta cut him off in turn. "We know full well if they wanted it, they would take it. They want to work together on this. Cassidy has convinced Flight Director Spear that she should work with us instead of demanding things of us, and it starts with this."

Margaretta was very firm, leaving no room for Carlson to argue, although it was obvious he wanted to.

"Myself, Cassidy, and one other – I suggest Olisker or Sasamuel – will go with members of the base to the pool and develop a plan for how they can recover the stone they need. Which one of you will go with us to help speak on behalf of the village?"

Olisker looked less than confident, but that was not unusual as he was still trying to get used to being a storyteller. Sasamuel was about to say something when Gertrand cut in.

"I think Olisker should go. Then he can help develop the story of this. This is a pivotal moment and will need to be told." She looked at Sasamuel. "You have created a few stories already, of course."

Sasamuel responded to the elder, "I was going to recommend Olisker. My days of going to the pool, I think, are over. It is time for the young people to create."

Gertrand smiled at him, and at Carlson, who looked

even sourer that he was not part of the decision making. Margaretta snickered a little and mumbled something about the pool creating many things.

***

The hike to the pool was uneventful. Margaretta and Olisker led as they already knew a better route as compared to the one Cassidy and Trice took. There was actually a nice, well-worn path to the area, used by generations of villagers to sneak away when courting.

Margaretta was still amazed. "I can't believe no one ever thought to go behind the waterfall! I know the water is icy all year round, but no one would ever swim in it?!"

Olisker joked. "Really Margaretta? If you ever came out here, were you really thinking of swimming? In the cold?"

Margaretta blushed and Trice laughed. "Sounds like the water is cold enough to destroy any chance of affection!"

Shari, shot them a look and rolled her eyes, but was happy to have the easy route.

Once at the pool, Trice once again confirmed just how cold the water was by sticking his hand in. Then he suggested they sidle along the cliff-face the way he and Cassidy had. They each followed, trying to balance small lanterns so they would be able to see. Inside, Shari was thrilled with the amount of material available, and Margaretta and Olisker were amazed to look down on the other side of the cavern and see where Ishaul must have found the first large stone. They tossed a couple of stones out of the cave to try to find later and finally know where the story took place.

Once out by the pool again, Shari conferred with Margaretta and Olisker.

"We will need to build a walkway to get to the waterfall. If we are going to take out a substantial amount, we will need to be able to carry it safely," explained Shari.

"I agree, and that is agreeable, but what is a substantial amount?" Margaretta asked.

"For now, let's say two of the large boulders in the front of the cavern," Shari said.

"Instead," Margaretta countered, "let's leave the boulders in the very front. There are others just behind by a few large steps. Take from there first and work back. That should maintain the way the waterfall cascades."

Shari considered. "I would never have thought of that, but there's no reason why we can't approach it that way."

Olisker broke in, "And when you say for now, what does that mean?"

Shari looked to him. "It would mean that we see how many aeroplanes we can alter, and how much nav equipment we can change with that much before taking any more. So far, we have altered six aeroplanes and a dozen or so handheld navs with just what people from your village gave you."

"So two boulders is a significant amount?" asked Olisker.

"It is, but should last a very long time," responded Shari.

Margaretta asked, "Could we draw up some form of contract for the future that says we have to be consulted before the removal of more material, but that we won't counter the request without cause?"

"Sounds fair," said Shari.

Cassidy knew this was something for them to work out, but also knew that such a contract could be difficult to enforce in the future. But it was not her place to negotiate. She had done enough damage, and Margaretta, Olisker, and Shari seemed happy to mend that for the time being.

Once everyone was in agreement about the place and how it would be used, the group went back to the village. In a surprising move, Margaretta invited Shari to the evening meal, and she accepted. It was the first time she had spent any significant time among the villagers, and conversation was slow at first, but soon the villagers were as welcoming to Shari as they had been to Cassidy when she first arrived.

***

"I am sorry to see you leave. It was lovely to speak to someone from the other side of the door."

Phia pulled Cassidy into a hug. When she let go, it was Margaretta's turn for a hug.

"The storytellers asked me to give you something," she said and handed Cassidy a small fragment of stone on a cord. "I know you have pieces of the stone to bring back, but this one is for you."

Cassidy put it on.

"Thank you so much, you have all been very friendly." Cassidy turned to Phia. "Do you have the note I gave you?"

"Yes, of course. I will use this as an introduction for

when people come through."

"Remember, there is always a chance that not everyone who comes through will be able to read, or be able to read that language. Most do, but this area of the world has a few different languages."

"I understand, but this should help quite a bit."

Cassidy had written out a note of greeting, explaining that the village would offer a place of comfort when it was needed and share their food. It also asked, if people were willing or able, for things they couldn't get, such as charcoal. It also asked that they tell a villager when they are leaving, so they could be given a care package of food and other supplies before they go.

"Are you sure it isn't unkind to ask for these wonderful items that you have in your world?" Phia asked.

"There's no harm in asking, as long as you're not demanding. Many of the people who come through are ones who have very little, but will likely be generous with what they do have," Cassidy explained. "And I will drop some things through the door before I go back to my own home."

"I thank you again, Cassidy. Are you certain you don't want your own package of food to take with you?" asked Margaretta.

"No, thank you. Save that for someone else."

In all honesty, Cassidy was looking forward to stopping at the convenience store for some chocolate and familiar food.

"Please say goodbye to Rim for me, and the storytellers."

"We will," Phia smiled. "Have a safe journey."

With that, Cassidy turned and walked through the space in the woods that was just a little different, and was greeted with the chill of the September air. Time was a little different, and in her week in the village, August had passed to September and the air had lost that last trace of summer. The air caught in Cassidy's lungs, making her breathe a little deeper. She felt like she had to suck the oxygen out of the air, and not just breathe casually. Cassidy walked to the corner store and bought herself a snack. She was a little out of breath from the walk, and guessed it would take her a little while to get used to the heaviness of the air again. She could better understand why the people from the village couldn't come through anymore as she felt like she could taste the exhaust and pollution on the wind after being in such a pristine place. Perhaps some of their knowledge of energy supplies would be more helpful for this planet, but Gamgee wanted a magnetic rock. She did think of the small sliver of halfstone in her bag.

She asked the clerk at the convenience store to call a taxi, which took her to an outdoor shop where she bought some camping gear, including a couple of bags of charcoal. She took another taxi back to the door and passed most of the items through. She had picked up a sleeping bag, which she left in the lean-to near the door for whoever was using it. From there, she walked up the road to a motel and checked in for the night.

Once in the room, she plugged in her phone to get her messages, sent a quick email to Dr. Gamgee, and called her family to check in. They were used to her disappearing, and were surprised when she called so soon after a field season. To be fair, they thought she was just back in service range from her excavation.

She laid the two samples of the mineral on the hotel desk, one covered in the white quartz-like layer, and the other just black. She put the piece of halfstone on the desk next to them. Tomorrow she would book a flight home, and deliver these to Dr. Gamgee. For tonight, she would catch up on emails and social media, and head down to the motel restaurant for a pile of fried foods she could name.

EPILOGUE

Margaretta writes in one of her books. The nib of her pen slows across the page, pausing only to collect more ink to continue the story. She is the keeper of the tales. While stories are told, and are meant to be told, they are also recorded in the library. Over the years, as stories change, they are recorded again, and again. The library has new stories, old stories, and how stories evolve over the generations. She inherited the library from Gertrand, and one day she will pass the library on to a new storyteller. Right now, she writes Olisker's story of the woman who came through the door.

One day, a woman came through the door. It was the wrong time of year. People come through the door in the warm season, but it was just after the rainy season. The woman, Cassidy, who came through the door could speak our language thanks to science from another world. She said she was looking for something to bring back to her world. We welcomed her, as we welcome all visitors who come through the door. We gave her shelter, a place to sleep, and food. She was different, because we gave her conversation and she gave us knowledge. She was welcomed, and we showed her the village and could tell how things are done in the village. It was a pleasure to talk to someone from through the door. She told us about her world.

The woman, Cassidy, came through the door during the Great Conflict, when the world was fighting. Cassidy spoke to the village, and to the military base. She shared information between the two groups. She shared that our idol, carved by Ishaul and brought to the village from somewhere unknown on the island, could help stop the aeroplanes from crashing on the island. She tried to bring the village and the base together, but the leader of the base stole the idol to help protect the soldiers and the aeroplanes.

The woman, Cassidy, left the village to talk to the leader of the base. In her time trying to retrieve the idol, she was taken around the island in an aeroplane, but like many others, the aeroplane crashed. Cassidy and the pilot survived an aeroplane crash and as they walked back to the village from deep in the forest, they came to the pool. The people of the village knew the pool, they would spend time there in the warm months, enjoying each other's company on the bank of the cold pond. Cassidy explored the pool, and went behind the waterfall. Behind the waterfall were stones like that found by Ishaul many generations ago.

The woman, Cassidy, brought a stone back to the village, and brought the leader of the base to the village. Together, the storytellers and the leader of the base shared the pool and the stones. The aeroplanes could fly safely, and the village gained the knowledge of where Ishaul found the idol. Cassidy, having brought the village and the base together, left, back through the door.

Margaretta knew there was more to the story, but stories didn't always need all of the details. This one was good, for Olisker's first story. More would come, and they would get better. And this story would change, but they would always remember the woman who came through the door and found Ishaul's secret place.

ACKNOWLEDGEMENTS

The authors would like to pay special thanks to the *Slipstreamers* committee at Engen Books, including Amanda Labonté, Matthew LeDrew, AJ Ryan, Ellen Curtis, Erin Vance, and, Lauralana Dunne.

Without their tireless efforts, none of this would have been possible.

Special thanks to this episode's editor, Ali House.

Lisa M Daly would also like to thank Shannon Green and Bronwynn Erskine for support and being available to listen and help with ideas. Finally, thanks to the participants at the Writer's Alliance of Newfoundland and Labrador writer's nights and members of Genre Writers of Atlantic Canada, who have given the author the confidence to even attempt such a project.

Lisa Daly would like to dedicate her part of the narrative to "Shannon and our cats, for all their support and company while I wrote."

Land Acknowledgement

Part of this story takes place along the Wolastoq, also known by the settler name of the Saint John River. This land is the traditional unceded territory of the Wəlastəkwiyik (Maliseet) Peoples. This territory is covered by the "Treaties of Peace and Friendship" which Wəlastəkwiyik (Maliseet), Mi'kmaq and Passamaquoddy Peoples first signed with the British Crown in 1726. The treaties did not deal with surrender of lands and resources but in fact recognized Mi'kmaq and Wəlastəkwiyik (Maliseet) title and established the rules for what was to be an ongoing relationship between nations. While the characters portrayed in this work are fictional, it is acknowledged that they would have been the ancestors of the modern-day Maliseet.

ON SALE NOW FROM ENGEN BOOKS

"Dunne breathes life into a world of magic and lore that will draw the reader in right up to the epic conclusion. Ashes is a heroic tale not to be missed."
Amanda Labonté
bestselling author of Supenatural Causes

When fifteen-year-old Phoenix loses her caregiver, everyone that she has ever known inexplicably turn their backs on her. Given the impossible burden of repaying an unknown debt, Phoenix sets out on her own with her trusty donkey, Muler, as her only companion.A chance encounter with Malcourt, a mysterious traveller, not only saves her life, but sets it on a trajectory that she would have never thought possible.

COMING SOON!
FLOWERS FOR ALBATROSS
BY JD RYOT & MATTHEW DANIELS!

The next incredible episode of Slipstreamers, *Flowers for Albatross*, will be available soon, written with the astonishing Matthew Daniels!

While exploring portals, Cassidy finds her strangest world yet: a world populated completely with dinosaurs! Warring factions of the great beasts each seek to recruit her, and she must navigate this tense world and find her path back home before the portal closes forever!

ABOUT THE AUTHOR

A native Newfoundlander, **Lisa M Daly** is an archaeologist, historian, professional ballroom dance instructor, crafter, and avid baker.

Previous non-fiction writing credits include essays *Sacrifice in Second World War Gander* and *An Empty Graveyard: The Victims of the 1946 AOA DC-4 Crash, Their Final Resting Place, and Dark Tourism.*

She made her fiction writing debut with 'The Island Outside the War' in *Dystopia from the Rock.*

Lisa acted as the guest editor for the Summer 2019 *Flights from the Rock* collection.

Navigating Stories is her first novella.

JD Ryot is the reclusive creator of the *Slipstreamers* series from Engen Books. JD is an avid fan of young adult literature and adventure serials. When asked if they had come to this world through a portal themselves, JD Ryot refused to answer. No record of their birth has ever been found... on this world.

www.ingramcontent.com/pod-product-compliance
Lightning Source LLC
LaVergne TN
LVHW051002080826
845145LV00009B/2421